The Holy Cross & Other Tales by Eugene Field

Eugene Field was born on 2nd September 1850 in St. Louis, Missouri. His mother died when he was six and his father when he was nineteen. His academic life was not taken seriously and he preferred the life of a prankster until, in 1875, he began work as a journalist for the St. Joseph Gazette in Saint Joseph, Missouri.

In his career as a journalist he soon found a niche that suited him. His articles were light, humorous and written in a personal gossipy style that endeared him to his readership. Some were soon being syndicated to other newspapers around the States. Field soon rose to city editor of the Gazette.

Field had first published poetry in 1879, when his poem 'Christmas Treasures' appeared. This was the beginning that would eventually number over a dozen volumes. As well as verse Field published an extensive range of short stories including 'The Holy Cross' and 'Daniel and the Devil.'

In 1889 whilst the family were in London and Field himself was recovering from a bout of ill health he wrote his most famous poem; 'Lovers Lane'.

On 4th November 1895 Eugene Field Sr died in Chicago of a heart attack at the age of 45.

Index of Contents

INTRODUCTION

ALAS, POOR YORICK!

In paying a tribute to the mingled mirth and tenderness of Eugene Field—the poet of whose going the West may say, "He took our daylight with him"—one of his fellow journalists has written that he was a jester, but not of the kind that Shakespeare drew in Yorick. He was not only—so the writer implied—the maker of jibes and fantastic devices, but the bard of friendship and affection, of melodious lyrical conceits; he was the laureate of children—dear for his "Wynken, Blynken and Nod" and "Little Boy Blue"; the scholarly book-lover, withal, who relished and paraphrased his Horace, who wrote with delight a quaint archaic English of his special devising; who collected rare books, and brought out his own "Little Books" of "Western Verse" and "Profitable Tales" in high-priced limited editions, with broad margins of paper that moths and rust do not corrupt, but which tempts bibliomaniacs to break through and steal.

For my own part, I would select Yorick as the very forecast, in imaginative literature, of our various Eugene. Surely Shakespeare conceived the "mad rogue" of Elsinore as made up of grave and gay, of wit and gentleness, and not as a mere clown or "jig maker." It is true that when Field put on his cap and bells, he too was "wont to set the table on a roar," as the feasters at a hundred tables, from "Casey's Table d'Hôte" to the banquets of the opulent East, now rise to testify. But Shakespeare plainly reveals, concerning Yorick, that mirth was not his sole attribute—that his motley covered the sweetest nature and the tenderest heart. It could be no otherwise with one who loved and comprehended childhood and whom the children loved. And what does Hamlet say?—"He hath borne me upon his back a thousand times . . . Here hung those lips that I have kissed I know not how oft!" Of what is he thinking but of his boyhood, before doubts and contemplation wrapped him in the shadow, and when in his young grief or frolic the gentle Yorick, with his jest, his "excellent fancy," and his songs and gambols, was his comrade?

Of all moderns, then, here or in the old world, Eugene Field seems to be most like the survival, or revival, of the ideal jester of knightly times; as if Yorick himself were incarnated, or as if a superior bearer of the bauble at the court of Italy, or of France, or of English King Hal, had come to life again—as much out of time as Twain's Yankee at the Court of Arthur; but not out of place—for he fitted himself as aptly to his folk and region as Puck to the fays and mortals of a wood near Athens. In the days of divine sovereignty, the jester, we see, was by all odds the wise man of the palace; the real fools were those he made his butt—the foppish pages, the obsequious courtiers, the swaggering guardsmen, the insolent nobles, and not seldom majesty itself. And thus it is that painters and romancers have loved to draw him. Who would not rather be Yorick than Osric, or Touchstone than Le Beau, or even poor Bertuccio than one of his brutal mockers? Was not the redoubtable Chicot, with his sword and brains, the true ruler of France? To come to the jesters of history—which is so much less real than fiction—what laurels are greener than those of Triboulet, and Will Somers, and John Heywood—dramatist and master of the king's merry Interludes? Their shafts were feathered with mirth and song, but pointed with wisdom, and well might old John Trussell say "That it often happens that wise counsel is more sweetly followed when it is tempered with folly, and earnest is the less offensive if it be delivered in jest."

Yes, Field "caught on" to his time—a complex American, with the obstreperous bizarrerie of the frontier and the artistic delicacy of our oldest culture always at odds within him—but he was, above all, a child of nature, a frolic incarnate, and just as he would have been in any time or country. Fortune had given him that unforgettable mummer's face—that clean-cut, mobile visage—that animated natural mask! No one else had so deep and rich a voice for the rendering of the music and pathos of a poet's lines, and no actor ever managed both face and voice better than he in delivering his own verses merry or sad. One night, he was seen among the audience at "Uncut Leaves," and was instantly requested to do something towards the evening's entertainment. As he was not in evening dress, he refused to take the platform, but stood up in the lank length of an ulster, from his corner seat, and recited "Dibdin's Ghost" and "Two Opinions" in a manner which blighted the chances of the readers that came after him. It is true that no clown ever equalled the number and lawlessness of his practical jokes. Above all, every friend that he had—except the Dean of his profession, for whom he did exhibit unbounded and filial reverence—was soon or late a victim of his whimsicality, or else justly distrusted the measure of Field's regard for him. Nor was the friendship perfected until one bestirred himself to pay Eugene back in kind. As to this, I am only one of scores now speaking from personal experience. There seemed to be no doubt in his mind that the victim of his fun, even when it outraged common sensibilities, must enjoy it as much as he. Who but Eugene, after being the welcome guest, at a European capital, of one of our most ambitious and refined ambassadors, would have written a lyric, sounding the praises of a German "onion pie," ending each stanza with

Ach, Liebe! Ach, mein Gott! and would have printed it in America, with his host's initials affixed?

My own matriculation at Eugene's College of Unreason was in this wise. In 1887, Mr. Ben Ticknor, the Boston publisher, was complaining that he needed some new and promising authors to enlarge his book-list. The New York "Sun" and "Tribune" had been copying Field's rhymes and prose extravaganzas—the former often very charming, the latter the broadest satire of Chicago life and people. I suggested to Mr. Ticknor that he should ask the poet-humorist to collect, for publication in book-form, the choicest of his writings thus far. To make the story brief, Mr. Field did so, and the outcome—at which I was somewhat taken aback—was the remarkable book, "Culture's Garland," with its title imitated from the sentimental "Annuals" of long ago, and its cover ornamented with sausages linked together as a coronal wreath! The symbol certainly fitted the greater part of the contents, which ludicrously scored the Chicago "culture" of that time, and made Pullman, Armour, and other commercial magnates of the Lakeside City special types in illustration. All this had its use, and many of the sufferers long since became the farceur's devoted friends. The Fair showed the country what Chicago really was and is. Certainly there is no other American city where the richest class appear so enthusiastic with respect to art and literature. "The practice of virtue makes men virtuous," and even if there was some pretence and affectation in the culture of ten years ago, it has resulted in as high standards of taste as can elsewhere be found. Moreover, if our own "four hundred" had even affected, or made it the fashion to be interested in, whatever makes for real culture, the intellectual life of this metropolis would not now be so far apart from the "social swim." There were scattered through "Culture's Garland" not a few of Field's delicate bits of verse. In some way he found that I had instigated Mr. Ticknor's request, and, although I was thinking solely of the publisher's interests, he expressed unstinted gratitude. Soon afterwards I was delighted to receive from him a quarto parchment "breviary," containing a dozen ballads, long and short, engrossed in his exquisitely fine handwriting, and illuminated with colored borders and drawings by the poet himself. It must have required days for the mechanical execution, and certainly I would not now exchange it for its weight in diamonds. This was the way our friendship began. It was soon strengthened by meetings and correspondence, and never afterwards broken.

Some years ago, however, I visited Chicago, to lecture, at the invitation of its famous social and literary "Twentieth Century Club." This was Eugene's opportunity, and I ought not to have been as dumfounded as I was, one day, when our evening papers copied from the "Chicago Record" a "very pleasant joke" at the expense of his town and myself! It was headed: "Chicago Excited! Tremendous Preparations for His Reception," and went on to give the order and route of a procession that was to be formed at the Chicago station and escort me to my quarters—stopping at Armour's packing-yards and the art-galleries on the way. It included the "Twentieth Century Club" in carriages, the "Browning Club" in busses, and the "Homer Club" in drays; ten millionnaire publishers, and as many pork-packers, in a chariot drawn by white horses, followed by not less than two hundred Chicago poets afoot! I have no doubt that Eugene thought I would enjoy this kind of advertisement as heartily as he did. If so, he lacked the gift of putting himself in the other man's place. But his sardonic face, a-grin like a school-boy's, was one with two others which shone upon me when I did reach Chicago, and my pride was not wounded sufficiently to prevent me from enjoying the restaurant luncheon to which he bore me off in triumph. I did promise to square accounts with him, in time, and this is how I fulfilled my word. The next year, at a meeting of a suburban "Society of Authors," a certain lady-journalist was chaffed as to her acquaintanceship with Field, and accused of addressing him as "Gene." At this she took umbrage, saying: "It's true we worked together on the same paper for five years, but he was always a perfect gentleman. I never called him 'Gene.'" This was reported by the press, and gave me the refrain for a skit entitled "Katharine and Eugenio:"

Five years she sate a-near him
Within that type-strewn loft;
She handed him the paste-pot,
He passed the scissors oft;
They dipped in the same inkstand
That crowned their desk between,
Yet—he never called her Katie,
She never called him "Gene."

Though close—ah! close—the droplight
That classic head revealed,
She was to him Miss Katharine,
He—naught but Mister Field;
Decorum graced his upright brow
And thinned his lips serene,
And, though he wrote a poem each hour,
Why should she call him "Gene?"

She gazed at his sporadic hair—
She knew his hymns by rote;
They longed to dine together
At Casey's table d'hôte;
Alas, that Fortune's "hostages"—
But let us draw a screen!
He dared not call her Katie;
How could she call him "Gene?"

I signed my verses "By one of Gene's Victims"; they appeared in The Tribune, and soon were copied by papers in every part of the country. Other stanzas, with the same refrain, were added by the funny men of the southern and western press, and it was months before 'Gene' saw the last of them. The word "Eugenio," which was the name by which I always addressed him in our correspondence, left him in no doubt as to the initiator of the series, and so our "Merry War" ended, I think, with a fair quittance to either side.

Grieving, with so many others, over Yorick's premature death, it is a solace for me to remember how pleasant was our last interchange of written words. Not long ago, he was laid very low by pneumonia, but recovered, and before leaving his sickroom wrote me a sweetly serious letter—with here and there a sparkle in it—but in a tone sobered by illness, and full of yearning for a closer companionship with his friends. At the same time he sent me the first editions, long ago picked up, of all my earlier books, and begged me to write on their fly-leaves. This I did; with pains to gratify him as much as possible, and in one of the volumes wrote this little quatrain:

TO EUGENE FIELD

Death thought to claim you in this year of years,
But Fancy cried—and raised her shield between—
"Still let men weep, and smile amid their tears;
Take any two beside, but spare Eugene!"

In view of his near escape, the hyperbole, if such there was, might well be pardoned, and it touched Eugene so manifestly that—now that the eddy indeed has swept him away, and the Sabine Farm mourns for its new-world Horace—I cannot be too thankful that such was my last message to him.

Eugene Field was so mixed a compound that it will always be impossible quite to decide whether he was wont to judge critically of either his own conduct or his literary creations. As to the latter, he put the worst and the best side by side, and apparently cared alike for both. That he did much beneath his standard, fine and true at times—is unquestionable, and many a set of verses went the rounds that harmed his reputation. On the whole, I think this was due to the fact that he got his stated income as a newspaper poet and jester, and had to furnish his score of "Sharps and Flats" with more or less regularity. For all this, he certainly has left pieces, compact of the rarer elements, sufficient in number to preserve for him a unique place among America's most original characters, scholarly wits, and poets of brightest fancy. Yorick is no more! But his genius will need no chance upturning of his grave-turf for its remembrance. When all is sifted, its fame is more likely to strengthen than to decline.

EDMUND CLARENCE STEDMAN

THE HOLY CROSS

Whilst the noble Don Esclevador and his little band of venturesome followers explored the neighboring fastnesses in quest for gold, the Father Miguel tarried at the shrine which in sweet piety they had hewn out of the stubborn rock in that strangely desolate spot. Here, upon that serene August morning, the holy Father held communion with the saints, beseeching them, in all humility, to intercede with our beloved Mother for the safe guidance of the fugitive Cortes to his native shores, and for the divine protection of the little host, which, separated from the Spanish army, had wandered leagues to the northward, and had sought refuge in the noble mountains of an unknown land. The Father's devotions were, upon a sudden, interrupted by the approach of an aged man who toiled along the mountain-side path—a man so aged and so bowed and so feeble that he seemed to have been brought down into that place, by means of some necromantic art, out of distant centuries. His face was yellow and wrinkled like ancient parchment, and a beard whiter than Samite streamed upon his breast, whilst about his withered body and shrunken legs hung faded raiment which the elements had corroded and the thorns had grievously rent. And as he toiled along, the aged man continually groaned, and continually wrung his palsied hands, as if a sorrow, no lighter than his years, afflicted him.

"In whose name comest thou?" demanded the Father Miguel, advancing a space toward the stranger, but not in threatening wise; whereat the aged man stopped in his course and lifted his eyebrows, and regarded the Father a goodly time, but he spake no word.

"In whose name comest thou?" repeated the priestly man. "Upon these mountains have we lifted up the cross of our blessed Lord in the name of our sovereign liege, and here have we set down a tabernacle to the glory of the Virgin and of her ever-blessed son, our Redeemer and thine—whoso thou mayest be!"

"Who is thy king I know not," quoth the aged man, feebly; "but the shrine in yonder wall of rock I know; and by that symbol which I see therein, and by thy faith for which it stands, I conjure thee, as thou lovest both, give me somewhat to eat and to drink, that betimes I may go upon my way again, for the journey before me is a long one."

These words spake the old man in tones of such exceeding sadness that the Father Miguel, touched by compassion, hastened to meet the wayfarer, and, with his arms about him, and with whisperings of sweet comfort, to conduct him to a resting-place. Coarse food in goodly plenty was at hand; and it happily fortuned, too, that there was a homely wine, made by Pietro del y Saguache himself, of the wild grapes in which a neighboring valley abounded. Of these things anon the old man partook, greedily but silently, and all that while he rolled his eyes upon the shrine; and then at last, struggling to his feet, he made as if to go upon his way.

"Nay," interposed the Father Miguel, kindly; "abide with us a season. Thou art an old man and sorely spent. Such as we have thou shalt have, and if thy soul be distressed, we shall pour upon it the healing balm of our blessed faith."

"Little knowest thou whereof thou speakest," quoth the old man, sadly. "There is no balm can avail me. I prithee let me go hence, ere, knowing what manner of man I am, thou hatest me and doest evil unto me." But as he said these words he fell back again even then into the seat where he had sat, and, as through fatigue, his hoary head dropped upon his bosom.

"Thou art ill!" cried the Father Miguel, hastening to his side. "Thou shalt go no farther this day! Give me thy staff,"—and he plucked it from him.

Then said the old man: "As I am now, so have I been these many hundred years. Thou hast heard tell of me—canst thou not guess my name; canst thou not read my sorrow in my face and in my bosom? As thou art good and holy through thy faith in that symbol in yonder shrine, hearken to me, for I will tell thee of the wretch whom thou hast succored. Then, if it be thy will, give me thy curse and send me on my way."

Much marvelled the Father Miguel at these words, and he deemed the old man to be mad; but he made no answer. And presently the old man, bowing his head upon his hands, had to say in this wise:—

"Upon a time," he quoth, "I abided in the city of the Great King—there was I born and there I abided. I was of good stature, and I asked favor of none. I was an artisan, and many came to my shop, and my cunning was sought of many—for I was exceeding crafty in my trade; and so, therefore, speedily my pride begot an insolence that had respect to none at all. And once I heard a tumult in the street, as of the cries of men and boys commingled, and the clashing of arms and staves. Seeking to know the cause thereof, I saw that one was being driven to execution—one that had said he was the Son of God and the King of the Jews, for which blasphemy and crime against our people he was to die upon the cross. Overcome by the weight of this cross, which he bore upon his shoulders, the victim tottered in the street and swayed this way and that, as though each moment he were like to fall, and he groaned in sore agony. Meanwhile about him pressed a multitude that with vast clamor railed at him and scoffed him and smote him, to whom he paid no heed; but in his agony his eyes were alway uplifted to heaven, and his lips moved in prayer for them that so shamefully entreated him. And as he went his way to Calvary, it fortuned that he fell and lay beneath the cross right at my very door, whereupon, turning his eyes upon me as I stood over against him, he begged me that for a little moment I should bear up the weight of the cross whilst that he wiped the sweat from off his brow. But I was filled with hatred, and I spurned him with my foot, and I said to him: 'Move on, thou wretched criminal, move on. Pollute not my doorway with thy touch—move on to death, I command thee!' This was the answer I gave to him, but no succor at all. Then he spake to me once again, and he said: 'Thou, too, shalt move on, O Jew! Thou shalt move on forever, but not to death!' And with these words he bore up the cross again and went upon his way to Calvary.

"Then of a sudden," quoth the old man, "a horror filled my breast, and a resistless terror possessed me. So was I accursed forevermore. A voice kept saying always to me: 'Move on, O Jew! move on forever!' From home, from kin, from country, from all I knew and loved I fled; nowhere could I tarry—the nameless horror burned in my bosom, and I heard continually a voice crying unto me: 'Move on, O Jew! move on forever!' So, with the years, the centuries, the ages, I have fled before that cry and in that nameless horror; empires have risen and crumbled, races have been born and are extinct, mountains have been cast up and time hath levelled them—still I do live and still I wander hither and thither upon the face of the earth, and am an accursed thing. The gift of tongues is mine—all men I know, yet mankind knows me not. Death meets me face to face, and passes me by; the sea devours all other prey, but will not hide me in its depths; wild beasts flee from me, and pestilences turn their consuming breaths elsewhere. On and on and on I go—not to a home, nor to my people, nor to my grave, but evermore into the tortures of an eternity of sorrow. And evermore I feel the nameless horror burn within, whilst evermore I see the pleading eyes of him that bore the cross, and evermore I hear his voice crying: 'Move on, O Jew! move on forevermore!'"

"Thou art the Wandering Jew!" cried the Father Miguel.

"I am he," saith the aged man. "I marvel not that thou dost revolt against me, for thou standest in the shadow of that same cross which I have spurned, and thou art illumined with the love of him that went his way to Calvary. But I beseech thee bear with me until I have told thee all—then drive me hence if thou art so minded."

"Speak on," quoth the Father Miguel.

Then said the Jew: "How came I here I scarcely know; the seasons are one to me, and one day but as another; for the span of my life, O priestly man! is eternity. This much know you: from a far country I embarked upon a ship—I knew not whence 't was bound, nor cared I. I obeyed the voice that bade me go. Anon a mighty tempest fell upon the ship and overwhelmed it. The cruel sea brought peace to all but me; a many days it tossed and buffeted me, then with a cry of exultation cast me at last upon a shore I had not seen before, a coast far, far westward whereon abides no human thing. But in that solitude still heard I from within the awful mandate that sent me journeying onward, 'Move on, O Jew! move on;' and into vast forests I plunged, and mighty plains I traversed; onward, onward, onward I went, with the nameless horror in my bosom, and—that cry, that awful cry! The rains beat upon me; the sun wrought pitilessly with me; the thickets tore my flesh; and the inhospitable shores bruised my weary feet—yet onward I went, plucking what food I might from thorny bushes to stay my hunger, and allaying my feverish thirst at pools where reptiles crawled. Sometimes a monster beast stood in my pathway and threatened to devour me; then would I spread my two arms thus, and welcome death, crying: 'Rend thou this Jew in twain, O beast! strike thy kindly fangs deep into this heart—be not afeard, for I shall make no battle with thee, nor any outcry whatsoever!' But, lo, the beast would cower before me and skulk away. So there is no death for me; the judgment spoken is irrevocable; my sin is unpardonable, and the voice will not be hushed!"

Thus and so much spake the Jew, bowing his hoary head upon his hands. Then was the Father Miguel vastly troubled; yet he recoiled not from the Jew—nay, he took the old man by the hand and sought to soothe him.

"Thy sin was most heinous, O Jew!" quoth the Father; "but it falleth in our blessed faith to know that whoso repenteth of his sin, what it soever may be, the same shall surely be forgiven. Thy punishment hath already been severe, and God is merciful, for even as we are all his children, even so his tenderness to us is like unto the tenderness of a father unto his child—yea, and infinitely tenderer and sweeter, for who can estimate the love of our heavenly Father? Thou didst deny thy succor to the Nazarene when he besought it, yet so great compassion hath he that if thou but callest upon him he will forget thy wrong—leastwise will pardon it. Therefore be thou persuaded by me, and tarry here this night, that in the presence of yonder symbol and the holy relics our prayers may go up with thine unto our blessed Mother and to the saints who haply shall intercede for thee in Paradise. Rest here, O sufferer—rest thou here, and we shall presently give thee great comfort." The Jew, well-nigh fainting with fatigue, being persuaded by the holy Father's gentle words, gave finally his consent unto this thing, and went anon unto the cave beyond the shrine, and entered thereinto, and lay upon a bed of skins and furs, and made as if to sleep. And when he slept his sleep was seemingly disturbed by visions, and he tossed as doth an one that sees full evil things, and in that sleep he muttered somewhat of a voice he seemed to hear, though round about there was no sound whatsoever, save only the soft music of the pine-trees on the mountain-side. Meanwhile in the shrine, hewn out of those rocks, did the Father Miguel bow before the sacred symbol of his faith and plead for mercy for that same Jew that slumbered anear. And when, as the deepening blue mantle of night fell upon the hilltops and obscured the valleys round about, Don Esclevador and his sturdy men came clamoring along the mountain-side, the holy Father met them a way off and bade them have regard to the aged man that slept in yonder cave. But when he told them of that Jew and of his misery and of the secret causes thereof, out spake the noble Don Esclevador, full hotly—

"By our sweet Christ," he cried, "shall we not offend our blessed faith and do most impiously in the Virgin's sight if we give this harbor and this succor unto so vile a sinner as this Jew that hath denied our dear Lord!"

Which words had like to wrought great evil with the Jew, for instantly the other men sprang forward as if to awaken the Jew and drive him forth into the night. But the Father Miguel stretched forth his hands and commanded them to do no evil unto the Jew, and so persuasively did he set forth the godliness and the sweetness of compassion that presently the whole company was moved with a gentle pity toward that Jew. Therefore it befell anon, when night came down from the skies and after they had feasted upon their homely food as was their wont, that they talked of the Jew, and thinking of their own hardships and misfortunes (whereof it is not now to speak), they had all the more compassion to that Jew, which spake them passing fair, I ween.

Now all this while lay the Jew upon the bed of skins and furs within the cave, and though he slept (for he was exceeding weary), he tossed continually from side to side, and spoke things in his sleep, as if his heart were sorely troubled, and as if in his dreams he beheld grievous things. And seeing the old man, and hearing his broken speech, the others moved softly hither and thither and made no noise soever lest they should awaken him. And many an one—yes, all that valiant company bowed down that night before the symbol in the shrine, and with sweet reverence called upon our blessed Virgin to plead in the cause of that wretched Jew. Then sleep came to all, and in dreams the noble Don Esclevador saw his sovereign liege, and kneeled before his throne, and heard his sovereign liege's gracious voice; in dreams the heartweary soldier sailed the blue waters of the Spanish main, and pressed his native shore, and beheld once again the lovelight in the dark eyes of her that awaited him; in dreams the mountain-pines were kissed of the singing winds, and murmured drowsily and tossed their arms as do little children that dream of their play; in dreams the Jew swayed hither and thither, scourged by that nameless horror in his bosom, and seeing the pleading eyes of our dying Master, and hearing that awful mandate: "Move on, O Jew! move on forever!" So each slept and dreamed his dreams—all slept but the Father Miguel, who alone throughout the night kneeled in the shrine and called unto the saints and unto our Mother Mary in prayer. And his supplication was for that Jew; and the mists fell upon that place and compassed it about, and it was as if the heavens had reached down their lips to kiss the holy shrine. And suddenly there came unto the Jew a quiet as of death, so that he tossed no more in his sleep and spake no word, but lay exceeding still, smiling in his sleep as one who sees his home in dreams, or his mother, or some other such beloved thing.

It came to pass that early in the morning the Jew came from the cavern to go upon his way, and the Father Miguel besought him to take with him a goodly loaf in his wallet as wise provision against hunger. But the Jew denied this, and then he said: "Last night while I slept methought I stood once more in the city of the Great King—ay, in that very doorway where I stood, swart and lusty, when I spurned him that went his way to Calvary. In my bosom burned the terror as of old, and my soul was consumed of a mighty anguish. None of those that passed in that street knew me; centuries had ground to dust all my kin. 'O God!' I cried in agony, 'suffer my sin to be forgotten—suffer me to sleep, to sleep forever beneath the burden of the cross I sometime spurned!' As I spake these words there stood before me one in shining raiment, and lo! 't was he who bore the cross to Calvary! His eyes that had pleaded to me on a time now fell compassionately upon me, and the voice that had commanded me move on forever, now broke full sweetly on my ears: 'Thou shalt go on no more, O Jew, but as thou hast asked, so shall it be, and thou shalt sleep forever beneath the cross.' Then fell I into a deep slumber, and, therefrom but just now awaking, I feel within me what peace bespeaketh pardon for my sin. This day am I ransomed; so suffer me to go my way, O holy man."

So went the Jew upon his way, not groaningly and in toilsome wise, as was his wont, but eagerly, as goeth one to meet his bride, or unto some sweet reward. And the Father Miguel stood long, looking after him and being sorely troubled in mind; for he knew not what interpretation he should make of all these things. And anon the Jew was lost to sight in the forest.

But once, a little space thereafter, while that José Conejos, the Castilian, clambered up the yonder mountain-side, he saw amid the grasses there the dead and withered body of an aged man, and thereupon forthwith made he such clamor that Don Esclevador hastened thither and saw it was the Jew; and since there was no sign that wild beasts had wrought evil with him, it was declared that the Jew had died of age and fatigue and sorrow, albeit on the wrinkled face there was a smile of peace that none had seen thereon while yet the Jew lived. And it was accounted to be a most wondrous thing that, whereas never before had flowers of that kind been seen in those mountains, there now bloomed all round about flowers of the dye of blood, which thing the noble Don Esclevador took full wisely to be a symbol of our dear Lord's most precious blood, whereby not only you and I but even the Jew shall be redeemed to Paradise.

Within the spot where they had found the Jew they buried him, and there he sleeps unto this very day. Above the grave the Father Miguel said a prayer; and the ground of that mountain they adjudged to be holy ground; but over the grave wherein lay the Jew they set up neither cross nor symbol of any kind, fearing to offend their holy faith.

But that very night, when that they were returned unto their camp half a league distant, there arose a mighty tempest, and there was such an upheaval and rending of the earth as only God's hand could make; and there was a crashing and a groaning as if the world were smitten in twain, and the winds fled through the valleys in dismay, and the trees of the forest shrieked in terror and fell upon their faces. Then in the morning when the tempest ceased and all the sky was calm and radiant they saw that an impassable chasm lay between them and that mountain-side wherein the Jew slept the sleep of death; that God had traced with his finger a mighty gulf about that holy ground which held the bones of the transgressor. Between heaven and earth hung that lonely grave, nor could any foot scale the precipice that guarded it; but one might see that the spot was beautiful with kindly mountain verdure and that flowers of blood-red dye bloomed in that lonely place.

This was the happening in a summer-time a many years ago; to the mellow grace of that summer succeeded the purple glory of the autumn, and then came on apace the hoary dignity of winter. But the earth hath its resurrection too, and anon came the beauteous spring-time with warmth and scents and new life. The brooks leapt forth once more from their hiding-places, the verdure awaked, and the trees put forth their foliage. Then from the awful mountain peaks the snow silently and slowly slipped to the valleys, and in divers natural channels went onward and ever downward to the southern sea, and now at last 't was summer-time again and the mellow grace of August brooded over the earth. But in that yonder mountain-side had fallen a symbol never to be removed—ay, upon that holy ground where slept the Jew was stretched a cross, a mighty cross of snow on which the sun never fell and which no breath of wind ever disturbed. Elsewhere was the tender warmth of verdure and the sacred passion of the blood-red flowers, but over that lonely grave was stretched the symbol of him that went his way to Calvary, and in that grave slept the Jew.

Mightily marvelled Don Esclevador and his warrior host at this thing; but the Father Miguel knew its meaning; for he was minded of that vision wherein it was foretold unto the Jew that, pardoned for his sin, he should sleep forever under the burden of the cross he spurned. All this the Father Miguel showed unto Don Esclevador and the others, and he said: "I deem that unto all ages this holy symbol shall bear witness of our dear Christ's mercy and compassion. Though we, O exiled brothers, sleep in this foreign land in graves which none shall know, upon that mountain height beyond shall stretch the eternal witness to our faith and to our Redeemer's love, minding all that look thereon, not of the pains and the punishments of the Jew, but of the exceeding mercy of our blessed Lord, and of the certain eternal peace that cometh through his love!"

How long ago these things whereof I speak befell, I shall not say. They never saw—that Spanish host—they never saw their native land, their sovereign liege, their loved ones' faces again; they sleep, and they are dust among those mighty mountains in the West. Where is the grave of the Father Miguel, or of Don Esclevador, or of any of the valiant Spanish exiles, it is not to tell; God only knoweth, and the saints: all sleep in the faith, and their reward is certain. But where sleepeth the Jew all may see and know; for on that awful mountain-side, in a spot inaccessible to man, lieth the holy cross of snow. The winds pass lightly over that solemn tomb, and never a sunbeam lingereth there. White and majestic it lies where God's hands have placed it, and its mighty arms stretch forth as in a benediction upon the fleeting dust beneath.

So shall it bide forever upon that mountain-side, and the memory of the Jew and of all else human shall fade away and be forgotten in the surpassing glory of the love and the compassion of him that bore the redeeming burden to Calvary.

There was none other in the quiet valley so happy as the rose-tree—none other so happy unless perchance it was the thrush who made his home in the linden yonder. The thrush loved the rose-tree's daughter, and he was happy in thinking that some day she would be his bride. Now the rose-tree had many daughters, and each was beautiful; but the rose whom the thrush loved was more beautiful than her sisters, and all the wooers came wooing her until at last the fair creature's head was turned, and the rose grew capricious and disdainful. Among her many lovers were the south wind and the fairy Dewlove and the little elf-prince Beambright and the hoptoad, whom all the rest called Mr. Roughbrown. The hoptoad lived in the stone-wall several yards away; but every morning and evening he made a journey to the rose-tree, and there he would sit for hours gazing with tender longings at the beautiful rose, and murmuring impassioned avowals. The rose's disdain did not chill the hoptoad's ardor. "See what I have brought you, fair rose," he would say. "A beautiful brown beetle with golden wings and green eyes! Surely there is not in all the world a more delicious morsel than a brown beetle! Or, if you but say the word, I will fetch you a tender little fly, or a young gnat— see, I am willing to undergo all toils and dangers for your own sweet sake."

Poor Mr. Roughbrown! His wooing was very hopeless. And all the time he courted the imperious rose, who should be peeping at him from her home in the hedge but as plump and as sleek a little Miss Dormouse as ever you saw, and her eyes were full of envy.

"If Mr. Roughbrown had any sense," she said to herself, "he would waste no time on that vain and frivolous rose. He is far too good a catch for her."

The south wind was forever sighing and sobbing about. He lives, you know, very many miles from here. His home is beyond a great sea; in the midst of a vast desert there is an oasis, and it is among the palm-trees and the flowers of this oasis that the south wind abides. When spring calls from the North, "O south wind, where are you? Come hither, my sunny friend!" the south wind leaps from his couch in the far-off oasis, and hastens whither the spring-time calls. As he speeds across the sea the mermaids seek to tangle him in their tresses, and the waves try to twine their white arms about him; but he shakes them off and laughingly flies upon his way. Wheresoever he goes he is beloved. With their soft, solemn music the pine-trees seek to detain him; the flowers of earth lift up their voices and cry, "Abide with us, dear spirit,"—but to all he answers: "The spring-time calls me in the North, and I must hasten whither she calls." But when the south wind came to the rose-tree he would go no farther; he loved the rose, and he lingered about her with singing and sighing and protestations.

It was not until late in the evening that Dewlove and the elf-prince appeared. Just as the moon rolled up in the horizon and poured a broad streak of silver through the lake the three crickets went "Chirp-chirp, chirp-chirp, chirp-chirp," and then out danced Dewlove and Beambright from their hiding-places. The cunning little fairy lived under the moss at the foot of the oak-tree; he was no bigger than a cambric needle—but he had two eyes, and in this respect he had quite the advantage of the needle. As for the elf-prince, his home was in the tiny, dark subterranean passage which the mole used to live in; he was plump as a cupid, and his hair was long and curly, although if you force me to it I must tell you that the elf-prince was really no larger than your little finger—so you will see that so far as physical proportions were concerned Dewlove and Beambright were pretty well matched. Merry, merry fellows they were, and I should certainly fail most lamentably did I attempt to tell you how prettily they danced upon the greensward of the meadowlands throughout the summer nights. Sometimes the other fairies and elves joined them—delicate little lady fairies with gossamer wings, and chubby little lady elves clad in filmy spider webs—and they danced and danced and danced, while the three crickets went "Chirp-chirp, chirp-chirp, chirp-chirp," all night long. Now it was very strange—was it not?—that instead of loving one of these delicate little lady fairies, or one of these chubby little lady elves, both Dewlove and Beambright loved the rose. Yet, she was indeed very beautiful.

The thrush did not pester the rose with his protestations of love. He was not a particularly proud fellow, but he thought too much of the rose to vex her with his pleadings. But all day long he would perch in the thicket and sing his songs as only a thrush can sing to the beautiful rose he loves. He sung, we will say, of the forests he had explored, of the famous river he had once seen, of the dew which the rose loved, of the storm-king that slew the old pine and made his cones into a crown—he sung of a thousand things which we might not understand, but which pleased the rose because she understood them. And one day the thrush swooped down from the linden upon a monstrous devil's darning-needle that came spinning along and poised himself to stab the beautiful rose. Yes, like lightning the thrush swooped down on this murderous monster, and he bit him in two, and I am glad of it, and so are you if your heart be not wholly callous.

"How comes it," said the rose-tree to the thrush that day—"how comes it that you do not woo my daughter? You have shown that you love her; why not speak to her?"

"No, I will wait," answered the thrush. "She has many wooers, and each wooes her in his own way. Let me show her by my devotion that I am worthy of her, and then perchance she will listen kindly to me when I speak to her."

The rose-tree thought very strange of this; in all her experience of bringing out her fair daughters into society she had never before had to deal with so curious a lover as the thrush. She made up her mind to speak for him.

"My daughter," said she to the rose, "the thrush loves you; of all your wooers he is the most constant and the most amiable. I pray that you will hear kindly to his suit."

The rose laughed carelessly—yes, merrily—as if she heeded not the heartache which her indifference might cause the honest thrush.

"Mother," said the rose, "these suitors are pestering me beyond all endurance. How can I have any patience with the south wind, who is forever importuning me with his sentimental sighs and melancholy wheezing? And as for that old hoptoad, Mr. Roughbrown—why, it is a husband I want, not a father!"

"Prince Beambright pleases you, then?" asked the rose-tree.

"He is a merry, capering fellow," said the daughter, "and so is his friend Dewlove; but I do not fancy either. And as for the thrush who sends you to speak for him—why, he is quite out of the question, I assure you. The truth is, mother, that I am to fill a higher station than that of bride to any of these simple rustic folk. Am I not more beautiful than any of my companions, and have I not ambitions above all others of my kind?"

"Whom have you seen that you talk so vain-gloriously?" cried the rose-tree in alarm. "What flattery has instilled into you this fatal poison?"

"Have you not seen the poet who comes this way every morning?" asked the rose. "His face is noble, and he sings grandly to the pictures Nature spreads before his eyes. I should be his bride. Some day he will see me; he will bear me away upon his bosom; he will indite to me a poem that shall live forever!"

These words the thrush heard, and his heart sank within him. If his songs that day were not so blithe as usual it was because of the words that the rose had spoken. Yet the thrush sang on, and his song was full of his honest love.

It was the next morning that the poet came that way. He lived in the city, but each day he stole away from the noise and crowd of the city to commune with himself and with Nature in the quiet valley where bloomed the rose-tree, where the thrush sung, and where dwelt the fays and the elves of whom it has been spoken. The sun shone fiercely; withal the quiet valley was cool, and the poet bared his brow to the breeze that swept down the quiet valley from the lake over yonder.

"The south wind loves the rose! Aha, aha, foolish brother to love the rose!"

This was what the breeze said, and the poet heard it. Then his eyes fell upon the rose-tree and upon her blooming daughters.

"The hoptoad loves the rose! Foolish old Roughbrown to love the rose, aha, aha!"

There was a malicious squeakiness in this utterance—of course it came from that envious Miss Dormouse, who was forever peeping out of her habitation in the hedge.

"What a beautiful rose!" cried the poet, and leaping over the old stone-wall he plucked the rose from the mother-tree—yes, the poet bore away this very rose who had hoped to be the poet's bride.

Then the rose-tree wept bitterly, and so did her other daughters; the south wind wailed, and the old hoptoad gave three croaks so dolorous that if you had heard them you would have said that his heart was truly broken. All were sad—all but the envious dormouse, who chuckled maliciously, and said it was no more than they deserved.

The thrush saw the poet bearing the rose away, yet how could the fluttering little creature hope to prevail against the cruel invader? What could he do but twitter in anguish? So there are tragedies and heartaches in lives that are not human.

As the poet returned to the city he wore the rose upon his breast. The rose was happy, for the poet spoke to her now and then, and praised her loveliness, and she saw that her beauty had given him an inspiration.

"The rose despised my brother! Aha, aha, foolish rose—but she shall wither!"

It was the breeze that spake; far away from the lake in the quiet valley its voice was very low, but the rose heard and trembled.

"It's a lie," cried the rose. "I shall not die. The poet loves me, and I shall live forever upon his bosom."

Yet a singular faintness—a faintness never felt before—came upon the rose; she bent her head and sighed. The heat—that was all—was very oppressive, and here at the entrance to the city the tumult aroused an aggravating dust. The poet seemed suddenly to forget the rose. A carriage was approaching, and from the carriage leaned a lady, who beckoned to the poet. The lady was very fair, and the poet hastened to answer her call. And as he hastened the rose fell from his bosom into the hot highway, and the poet paid no heed. Ascending into the carriage with the lady (I am sure she must have been a princess!) the poet was whirled away, and there in the stifling dust lay the fainting rose, all stained and dying.

The sparrows flew down and pecked at her inquisitively; the cruel wagons crushed her beneath their iron wheels; careless feet buffeted her hither and thither. She was no longer a beautiful rose; no, nor even a reminiscence of one—simply a colorless, scentless, ill-shapen mass.

But all at once she heard a familiar voice, and then she saw familiar eyes. The voice was tender and the eyes were kindly.

"O honest thrush," cried the rose, "is it you who have come to reproach me for my folly?"

"No, no, dear rose," said the thrush, "how should I speak ill to you? Come, rest your poor head upon my breast, and let me bear you home."

"Let me rather die here," sighed the rose, "for it was here that my folly brought me. How could I go back with you whom I never so much as smiled upon? And do they not hate and deride me in the valley? I would rather die here in misery than there in shame!"

"Poor, broken flower, they love you," urged the thrush. "They grieve for you; let me bear you back where the mother-tree will shade you, and where the south wind will nurse you—for—for he loves you."

So the thrush bore back the withering rose to her home in the quiet valley.

"So she has come back, has she?" sneered the dormouse. "Well, she has impudence, if nothing else!"

"She was pretty once," said the old hoptoad; "but she lost her opportunity when I made up my mind to go wooing a certain glossy damsel in the hedge."

The rose-tree reached out her motherly arms to welcome her dying daughter, and she said: "Rest here, dear one, and let me rock you to repose."

It was evening in the quiet valley now. Where was the south wind that he came not with his wooing? He had flown to the North, for that day he had heard the spring-time's voice a-calling, and he went in answer to its summons. Everything was still. "Chirp-chirp, chirp-chirp, chirp-chirp," piped the three crickets, and forthwith the fairy boy and the elf-prince danced from their habitations. Their little feet tinkled over the clover and the daisies.

"Hush, little folk," cried the rose-tree. "Do not dance to-night—the rose is dying."

But they danced on. The rose did not hear them; she heard only the voice of the thrush, who perched in the linden yonder, and, with a breaking heart, sung to the dying flower.

THE PAGAN SEAL-WIFE

It is to tell of Harold, the son of Egbert, the son of Ib; comely was he to look upon, and a braver than he lived not in these islands, nor one more beloved of all people. But it chanced upon a time, while he was still in early manhood, that a grievous sorrow befell him; for on a day his mother Eleanor came to her end in this full evil wise. It was her intent to go unto the neighboring island, where grazed the goats and the kine, and it fortuned that, as she made her way thither in the boat, she heard sweet music, as if one played upon a harp in the waters, and, looking over the side of the boat, she beheld down in the waters a sea-maiden making those exceeding pleasant sounds. And the sea-maiden ceased to play, and smiled up at Eleanor, and stretched up her hands and besought Eleanor to pluck her from the sea into the boat, which seeking to do, Eleanor fell headlong into the waters, and was never thereafter seen either alive or dead by any of her kin. Now under this passing heavy grief Egbert, the son of Ib, being old and spent by toil, brake down, and on a night died, making with his latest breath most heavy lamentation for Eleanor, his wife; so died he, and his soul sped, as they tell, to that far northern land where the souls of the departed make merry all the night, which merriment sendeth forth so vast and so beautiful a light that all the heavens are illumined thereby. But Harold, the son of Egbert and of Eleanor, was left alone, having neither brother, nor sister, nor any of kin, save an uncle abiding many leagues distant in Jutland. Thereupon befell a wonderful thing; if it had not happened it would not be told. It chanced that, on a certain evening in the summer-time, Harold walked alone where a Druid circle lay coiled like a dark serpent on a hillside; his heart was filled with dolor, for he thought continually of Eleanor, his mother, and he wept softly to himself through love of that dear mother. While thus he walked in vast heaviness of soul, he was beheld of Membril, the fairy that with her goodly subjects dwelt in the ruin of the Pict's house hard by the Druid circle. And Membril had compassion upon Harold, and upon the exceeding fine down of a tiny sea-bird she rode out to meet him, and it was before his eyes as if a star shined out of a mist in his pathway. So it was that Membril the fairy made herself known to him, and having so done, she said and she sung:

I am Membril, queen of Fay,
That would charm thy grief away!
Thou art like the little bark
Drifting in the cold and dark—
Drifting through the tempest's roar
To a rocky, icy shore;
All the torment dost thou feel
Of the spent and fearful seal
Wounded by the hunter's steel.
I am Membril—hark to me:
Better times await on thee!
Wouldst thou clasp thy mother dear—
Strange things see and stranger hear?
Straight betake thee to thy boat
And to yonder haven float—
Go thy way, and silent be—
It is Membril counsels thee;
Go thy way, and thou shalt see!

Great marvel had Harold to this thing; nevertheless he did the bidding of Membril the fairy, and it was full wisely done. And presently he came to where his boat lay, half on the shore and half in the waters, and he unloosed the thong that held it, and entered into the boat; but he put neither hand to the oars thereof, for he was intent to do the bidding of Membril the fairy. Then as if of its own accord, or as if the kindly waves themselves bore it along, the boat moved upon the waters and turned toward the yonder haven whereof it was said and sung. Fair shone the moon, and the night was passing fair; the shadows fell from the hilltops in their sleep and lay, as they had been little weary children, in the valleys and upon the shore, and they were rocked in the cradles of those valleys, and the waters along the shore sung softly to them. Upon the one side lay the island where grazed the goats and the kine, and upon the other side lay the island where Harold and other people abode; between these islands crept the sea with its gentle murmurings, and upon this sea drifted the boat bearing Harold to the yonder haven. Now the haven whereunto the course lay brooded almost beneath the shadow of the Stennis stones, and the waters thereof were dark, as if, forsooth, the sea frowned whensoever it saw those bloody stones peering down into its tranquil bosom. And some said that the place was haunted, and that upon each seventh night came thereunto the spirits of them that had been slain upon those stones, and waved their ghostly arms and wailed grievously; but of latter times none believeth this thing to be true.

It befell that, coming into the haven and bearing toward the shore thereof, Harold was 'ware of sweet music, and presently he saw figures as of men and women dancing upon the holm; but neither could he see who these people were, nor could he tell wherefrom the music came. But such fair music never had he heard before, and with great marvel he came from the boat into the cluster of beech-trees that stood between the haven and that holm where the people danced. Then of a sudden Harold saw twelve skins lying upon the shore in the moonlight; and they were the comeliest and most precious sealskins that ever he saw, and he coveted them. So presently he took up one of the sealskins and bore it with him into his boat, and pushed the boat from the shore into the waters of the haven again, and, so doing, there was such plashing of the waters that those people dancing upon the fair green holm became 'ware of Harold's presence, and were afeared, so that, ceasing from their sport, they made haste down to the shore and did on the skins and dived into the waters with shrill cries. But there was one of them that could not do so, because Harold bore off that skin wherewith she was wont to begird herself, and when she found it not she wailed and wept and besought Harold to give her that skin again—and, lo! it was Eleanor, the wife of Egbert! Now when Harold saw that it was his mother that so entreated him he was filled with wonder, and he drew nearer the shore to regard her and to hear her words, for he loved her passing well. But he denied her that skin, knowing full well that so soon as she possessed it she would leave him and he should never again behold her. Then Eleanor related to him how that she had been drowned in the sea through treachery of the harp-maiden, and how that the souls of drowned people entered into the bodies of seals, nor were permitted to return to earth, save only one night in every month, at which time each recovered his human shape and was suffered to dance in the moonlight upon the fair green holm from the hour of sunset unto the hour of sunrise.

"Give me the skin, I pray thee," she cried, "for if the sun came upon me unawares I should crumble into dust before thine eyes, and that moment would a curse fall upon you. I am happy as I am; the sea and those who dwell therein are good to me—give me the skin, I beseech thee, that I may return whence I came, and thereby shall a great blessing accrue to thee and thine."

But Harold said: "Nay, mother, I were a fool to part so cheerfully with one whom I love dearer than life itself! I shall not let you go so easily; you shall come with me to our home, where I have lived alone too long already. I shall be alone no longer—come with me, I say, for I will not deliver up this skin, nor shall any force wrest it from me!"

Then Eleanor, his mother, reasoned a space with him, and anon she showed him the folly of his way; but still he hung his head upon his breast and was loath to do her bidding, until at last she sware unto him that if he gave to her that skin he should, upon the next dancing night, have to wife the most beautiful maiden in the world, and therefore should be alone in the world no more. To this presently Harold gave assent, and then Eleanor, his mother, bade him come to that same spot one month hence, and do what she should then bid him do. Receiving, therefore, the skin from him, she folded it about her and threw herself into the sea, and Harold betook himself unto his home.

Now wit ye well that full wearily dragged the days and the nights until that month was spent; but now at last it was the month of August, and upon the night of the seventh day thereof ended the season of waiting. It is to tell that upon that night came Harold, the son of Egbert, from his hut, and stood on the threshold thereof, and awaited the rising of the moon from out the silver waters yonder. While thus he stood there appeared unto him Membril the fairy, and smiling upon him she said and she sung:—

I am Membril, queen of Fay,
Come to urge thee on thy way;
Haste to yonder haven-side
Where awaits thy promised bride;
Daughter of a king is she—
Many leagues she comes to thee,
Thine and only thine to be.
Haste and see, then come again
To thy pretty home, and, when
Smiles the sun on earth once more,
Will come knocking at thy door;
Open then, and to thy breast
Clasp whom thou shalt love the best!
It is Membril counsels thee—
Haste and see what thou shalt see!

 Now by this thing was Harold mightily rejoiced, and he believed it to be truth that great good was in store for him; for he had seen pleasant things in the candle a many nights, and the smoke from his fire blew cheerily and lightly to the westward, and a swan had circled over his house that day week, and in his net each day for twice seven days had he drawn from the sea a fish having one golden eye and one silver eye: which things, as all men know, portend full goodly things, or else they portend nothing at all whatsoever. So, being pleasantly minded, Harold returned in kind unto Membril, the fairy queen, that bespoke him so courteously, and to her and to them that bore her company he said and he sung:—

Welcome, bonnie queen of Fay!
For thou speakest pleasing words;
Thou shalt have a gill of whey
And a thimblefull of curds;
In this rose is honey-dew
That a bee hath brought for you!

Welcome, bonnie queen of Fay!
Call thy sisters from the gloam,
And, whilst I am on my way,
Feast and frolic in my home—
Kiss the moonbeams, blanching white,
Shrinking, shivering with affright!

Welcome, all, and have no fear—
There is flax upon the sill,
No foul sprite can enter here—
Feast and frolic as you will;
Feast and frisk till break of day—

Welcome, little folk of Fay!

Thus having said and thus having sung, Harold went upon his way, and came to his boat and entered into it and journeyed to the haven where some time he had seen and discoursed with Eleanor, his mother. His course to this same haven lay, as before, over the waters that stole in between the two islands from the great sea beyond. Fair shone the moon, and the night was passing fair; the shadows rolled from the hilltops in their sleep and lay like little weary children in the valleys and upon the shore, and they were rocked in the cradles of those valleys, and the waters along the shore sung softly to them. Upon this hand lay the island where the goats and the kine found sweet pasturage, and upon the other hand stretched the island where people abode, and where the bloody Stennis stones rebuked the smiling sky, and where ghosts walked and wailed and waved their white arms in the shadows of those haunted ruins where once upon a time the Picts had dwelt. And Harold's heart was full of joy, the more in especial when, as he bore nigh unto the haven, he heard sweet music and beheld a goodly company of people that danced in the moonlight upon the fair green holm. Then, when presently his boat touched the inner shore of the haven, and he departed therefrom and drew the boat upon the shore, he saw wherefrom issued the beautiful music to which the people danced; he saw that the waters reached out their white fingers and touched the kale and the fair pebbles and the brittle shells and the moss upon the beach, and these things gave forth sweet sounds, which were as if a thousand attuned harps vied with the singing of the summer-night winds. Then, as before, Harold saw sealskins lying upon the shore, and presently came Eleanor, his mother, and pointing to a certain fair velvet skin, she said: "Take that fair velvet skin into thy boat and speed with all haste to thy home. To-morrow at sunrise thy bride shall come knocking at thy door. And so, farewell, my son—oh, Harold, my only son!" Which saying, Eleanor, the wife of Egbert, drew a skin about her and leapt into the sea; nor was she ever thereafter beholden of human eyes.

Then Harold took up the fair velvet skin to which his mother had directed him, and he bore it away with him in his boat. So softly went he upon the waters that none of them that danced upon the fair green holm either saw or heard him. Still danced they on to the sweet music made by the white fingers of the waves, and still shone the white moon upon the fair green holm where they so danced.

Now when came Harold to his home, bearing the precious skin with him, he saw the fairies at play upon the floor of his hut, and they feared no evil, for there was barley strewn upon the sill so that no wicked sprite could enter there. And when Membril, the fairy queen, saw him bringing the skin that he had found upon the shore, she bade him good welcome, and she said and she sung:—

I am Membril, queen of Fay—
Ponder well what words I say;
Hide that fair and velvet skin
Some secluded spot within;
In the tree where ravens croak—
In the hollow of the oak,
In the cave with mosses lined,
In the earth where none may find;
Hide it quick and hide it deep—
So secure shall be thy sleep,
Thine shall bride and blessings be,
Thine a fair posterity—
So doth Membril counsel thee!

So, pondering upon this counsel and thinking well of it, Harold took the fair velvet skin and hid it, and none knew where it was hid—none save only the raven that lived in the hollow oak. And when he had so done he returned unto his home and lay upon his bed and slept. It came to pass that early upon the morrow, when the sun made all the eastward sky blush for the exceeding ardor of his morning kiss, there came a knocking at the door of Harold's hut, and Harold opened the door, and lo! there stood upon the threshold the fairest maiden that eyes ever beheld. Unlike was she to maidens dwelling in those islands, for her hair was black as the waters of the long winter night, and her eyes were as the twin midnight rocks that look up from the white waves of the moonlit sea in yonder reef; withal was she most beautiful to look upon, and her voice was as music that stealeth to one over pleasant waters.

The maiden's name was Persis, and she was the daughter of a Pagan king that ruled in a country many, many—oh, many leagues to the southward of these islands, in a country where unicorns and dragons be, and where dwelleth the phoenix and hippogriffins and the cockatrix, and where bloometh a tree that runneth blood, and where mighty princes do wondrous things. Now it fortuned that the king was minded to wed his daughter Persis unto a neighboring prince, a high and mighty prince, but one whom Persis loved not, neither could she love. So for the first time Persis said, "Nay, I will not," unto her father's mandate, whereat the king was passing wroth, and he put his daughter in a place that was like a jail to her, for it was where none might see her, and where she might see none—none but those that attended upon her. This much told Persis, the Pagan princess, unto Harold, and then, furthermore, she said: "The place wherein I was put by the king, my father, was hard by the sea, and oftentimes I went thereon in my little boat, and once, looking down from that boat into the sea, I saw the face of a fair young man within a magic mirror that was held up in the waters of the sea by two ghostly hands, and the fair young man moved his lips and smiled at me, and methought I heard him say: 'Come, be my bride, O fair and gentle Persis!' But, vastly afeared, I cried out and put back again to shore. Yet in my dreams I saw that face and heard that voice, nor could I find any rest until I came upon the sea again in hope to see the face and hear the voice once more. Then, that second time, as I looked into the sea, another face came up from below and lifted above the waters, and a woman's voice spake thus to me: 'I am mother of him that loveth thee and whom thou lovest; his face hast thou seen in the mirror, and of thee I have spoken to him; come, let me bear thee as a bride to him!' And in that moment a faintness came upon me and I fell into her arms, and so was I drowned (as men say), and so was I a seal a little space until last dancing night, when, lo! some one brought me to life again, and one that said her name was Membril showed me the way unto thy door. And now I look upon thy face in truth, and thou art he who shall have me to his wife, for thou art he whose face I saw within the mirror which the ghostly hands bore up to me that day upon the sea!"

Great then was Harold's joy, and he folded her in his arms, and he spake sweet words to her, and she was content. So they were wed that very day, and there came to do them honor all the folk upon these islands: Dougal and Tam and Ib and Robbie and Nels and Gram and Rupert and Rolf and many others and all their kin, and they made merry, and it was well. And never spake the Pagan princess of that soft velvet skin which Harold had hid away—never spake she of it to him or to any other one.

It is to tell that to Harold and to Persis were born these children, and in this order: Egbert and Ib (that was nicknamed the Strong) and Harold and Joan and Tam and Annie and Rupert the Fair and Flocken and Elsa and Albert and Theodoric—these eleven children were born unto them in good time; and right fair children were they to see, comely and stout, yet sweetly minded withal. And prosperous times continually befell Harold; his herds multiplied, and the fish came into his nets, so that presently there was none other richer than he in all that country, and he did great good with his riches, for he had compassion to the poor. So Harold was beloved of all, and all spake full fairly of his wife—how that she cared for his little ones, and kept the house, and did deeds of sweet charity among the needy and distressed—ay, so was Persis, the wife of Harold, beloved of all, and by none other more than by Harold, who was wont to say that Persis had brought him all he loved best: his children, his fortune, his happiness, and, best of all, herself. So now they were wed twice seven years, and in that time was Persis still as young and fair to look upon as when she came to Harold's door for the first time and knocked. This I account to be a marvel, but still more a marvel was it that in all these years spake she never a word of that soft velvet skin which Harold took and hid—never a word to him nor to any one else. But the soft velvet skin lay meanwhile in the hollow of the oak, and in the branches of that tree perched a raven that croaked and croaked and croaked.

Now it befell upon a time that a ship touched at that island, and there came therefrom men that knelt down upon the shore and made strange prayers to a strange God, and forthwith uplifted in that island a symbol of wood in the similitude of a cross. Straightway went Harold with the rest to know the cause thereof, being fearful lest for this impiety their own gods, whom they served diligently, should send hail and fire upon them and their herds. But those that had come in the ship spake gently with them and showed themselves to be peaceful folk whose God delighted not in wars, but rather in gentleness and love. How it was, I, knowing not, cannot say, but presently the cause of that new God, whose law was gentleness and love, waxed mightily, and the people came from all around to kiss that cross and worship it. And among them came Harold, for in his heart had dawned the light of a new wisdom, and he knew the truth as we know it, you and I. So Harold was baptized in the Christian faith, he and his children; but Persis, his wife, was not baptized, for she was the daughter of a Pagan king, and she feared to bring evil upon those she loved by doing any blasphemous thing. Right sorely grieved was Harold because of this, and oftentimes he spake with her thereof, and oftentimes he prayed unto his God and ours to incline her mind toward the cross, which saveth all alike. But Persis would say: "My best beloved, let me not do this thing in haste, for I fear to vex thy God since I am a Pagan and the daughter of a Pagan king, and therefore have not within me the light that there is in thee and thy kind. Perchance (since thy God is good and gracious) the light will come to me anon, and shine before mine eyes as it shineth before thine. I pray thee, let me bide my time." So spake Persis, and her life ever thereafter was kind and charitable, as, soothly, it had ever before been, and she served Harold, her husband, well, and she was beloved of all, and a great sweetness came to all out of her daily life.

It fortuned, upon a day whilst Harold was from home, there was knocking at the door of their house, and forthwith the door opened and there stood in the midst of them one clad all in black and of rueful countenance. Then, as if she foresaw evil, Persis called unto her little ones and stood between them and that one all in black, and she demanded of him his name and will. "I am the Death-Angel," quoth he, "and I come for the best-beloved of thy lambs!"

Now Theodoric was that best-beloved; for he was her very little one, and had always slept upon her bosom. So when she heard those words she made a great outcry, and wrestled with the Death-Angel, and sought to stay him in his purpose. But the Death-Angel chilled her with his breath, and overcame her, and prevailed against her; and he reached into the midst of them and took Theodoric in his arms and folded him upon his breast, and Theodoric fell asleep there, and his head dropped upon the Death-Angel's shoulder. But in her battle for the child, Persis catched at the chain about the child's neck, and the chain brake and remained in her hand, and upon the chain was the little cross of fair alabaster which an holy man had put there when Theodoric was baptized. So the Death-Angel went his way with that best-beloved lamb, and Persis fell upon her face and wailed.

The years went on and all was well upon these islands. Egbert became a mighty fisherman, and Ib (that was nicknamed the Strong) wrought wondrous things in Norroway, as all men know; Joan was wed to Cuthbert the Dane, and Flocken was wooed of a rich man's son of Scotland. So were all things for good and for the best, and it was a marvel to all that Persis, the wife of Harold, looked still to be as young and beautiful as when she came from the sea to be her husband's bride. Her life was full of gentleness and charity, and all folk blessed her. But never in all these years spake she aught to any one of the fair velvet skin; and through all the years that skin lay hid in the hollow of the oak-tree, where the raven croaked and croaked and croaked.

At last upon a time a malady fell upon Persis, and a strange light came into her eyes, and naught they did was of avail to her. One day she called Harold to her, and said: "My beloved, the time draweth near when we twain must part. I pray thee, send for the holy man, for I would fain be baptized in thy faith and in the faith of our children." So Harold fetched the holy man, and Persis, the daughter of the Pagan king, was baptized, and she spake freely and full sweetly of her love to Jesus Christ, her Saviour, and she prayed to be taken into his rest. And when she was baptized, there was given to her the name of Ruth, which was most fairly done, I trow, for soothly she had been the friend of all.

Then, when the holy man was gone, she said to her husband: "Beloved, I beseech thee go to yonder oak-tree, and bring me from the hollow thereof the fair velvet skin that hath lain therein so many years."

Then Harold marvelled, and he cried: "Who told thee that the fair velvet skin was hidden there?"

"The raven told me all," she answered; "and had I been so minded I might have left thee long ago— thee and our little ones. But I loved thee and them, and the fair velvet skin hath been unseen of me."

"And wouldst thou leave us now?" he cried. "Nay, it shall not be! Thou shalt not see that fair velvet skin, for this very day will I cast it into the sea!"

But she put an arm about his neck and said: "This night, dear one, we part; but whether we shall presently be joined together in another life I know not, neither canst thou say; for I, having been a Pagan and the daughter of a Pagan king, may by my birth and custom have so grievously offended our true God that even in his compassion and mercy he shall not find pardon for me. Therefore I would have thee fetch—since I shall die this night and do require of thee this last act of kindness—I would have thee fetch that same fair velvet skin from yonder oak-tree, and wrap me therein, and bear me hence, and lay me upon the green holm by the farther haven, for this is dancing night, and the seal-folk shall come from the sea as is their wont. Thou shalt lay me, so wrapped within that fair velvet skin, upon that holm, and thou shalt go a space aside and watch throughout the night, coming not anear me (as thou lovest me!) until the dawn breaks, nor shalt thou make any outcry, but thou shalt wait until the night is sped. Then, when thou comest at daybreak to the holm, if thou findest me in the fair velvet skin thou shalt know that my sin hath been pardoned; but if I be not there thou may'st know that, being a Pagan, the seal-folk have borne me back into the sea unto my kind. Thus do I require of thee; swear so to do, and let thy beloved bless thee."

So Harold swore to do, and so he did. Straightway he went to the oak-tree and took from the hollow thereof the fair velvet skin; seeing which deed, the raven flew away and was never thereafter seen in these islands. And with a heavy heart, and with full many a caress and word of love, did Harold bind his fair wife in that same velvet skin, and he bore her to his boat, and they went together upon the waters; for he had sworn so to do. His course unto the haven lay as before over the waters that stole in between the two islands from the great troubled sea beyond. Fair shone the moon, and the night was passing fair; the shadows lay asleep, like little weary children, in the valleys, and the waters moaned, and the winds rebuked the white fingers that stretched up from the waves to clutch them. And when they were come to the inner shore of the haven, Harold took his wife and bore her up the bank and laid her where the light came down from the moon and slept full sweetly upon the fragrant sward. Then, kissing her, he went his way and sat behind the Stennis stones a goodly space beyond, and there he kept his watch, as he had sworn to do.

Now wit ye well a grievous heavy watch it was that night, for his heart yearned for that beloved wife that lay that while upon the fair green holm—ay, never before had night seemed so long to Harold as did that dancing night when he waited for the seal-folk to come where the some-time Pagan princess lay wrapped in the fair velvet skin. But while he watched and waited, Membril, the fairy queen, came and brought others of her kind with her, and they made a circle about Harold, and threw around him such a charm that no evil could befall him from the ghosts and ghouls that in their shrouds walked among those bloody stones and wailed wofully and waved their white arms. For Membril, coming to Harold in the similitude of a glow-worm, made herself known to him, and she said and she sung:

Loving heart, be calm a space
In this gloomy vigil place;
Though these confines haunted be
Naught of harm can come to thee—
Nothing canst thou see or hear
Of the ghosts that stalk anear,
For around thee Membril flings
Charms of Fay and fairy rings.

Nothing daunted was Harold by thoughts of evil monsters, and naught recked he of the uncanny dangers of that haunted place; but he addressed these words to Membril and her host, and he said and he sung:

Tell me if thy piercing eyes
See the inner haven shore.
There my Own Beloved lies,
With the cowslips bending o'er:
Speed, O gentle folk of Fay!
And in guise of cowslips say
I shall love my love for aye!

Even so did Membril and the rest; and presently they returned, and they brought these words unto Harold, saying and singing them:—

We as cowslips in that place
Clustered round thy dear one's face,
And we whispered to her there
Those same words we went to bear;
And she smiled and bade us then
Bear these words to thee again:
"Die we shall, and part we may—
Love is love and lives for aye!"

Then of a sudden there was a tumult upon the waters, as if the waters were troubled, and there came up out of the waters a host of seals that made their way to the shore and cast aside their skins and came forth in the forms of men and of women, for they were the drowned folk that were come, as was their wont, to dance in the moonlight upon the fair green holm. At that moment the waters stretched out their white fingers and struck the kale and the pebbles and the soft moss upon the beach, for they sought to make music for the seal-folk to dance thereby; but the music that was made was not merry nor gleeful, but was passing gruesome and mournful. And presently the seal-folk came where lay the wife of Harold wrapped in the fair velvet skin, and they knew her of old, and they called her by what name she was known to them, "Persis! Persis!" over and over again, and there was great wailing among the seal-folk for a mighty space; and the seal-folk danced never at all that night, but wailed about the wife of Harold, and called "Persis! Persis!" over and over again, and made great moan. And at last all was still once more, for the seal-folk, weeping and clamoring grievously, went back into the sea, and the sea sobbed itself to sleep.

Mindful of the oath he swore, Harold dared not go down to that shore, but he besought Membril, the queen of Fay, to fetch him tidings from his beloved, whether she still lay upon the holm, or whether the seal-folk had borne her away with them into the waters of the deep. But Membril might not go, nor any of her host, for already the dawn was in the east and the kine were lowing on yonder slope. So Harold was left alone a tedious time, until the sun looked upon the earth, and then, with clamoring heart, Harold came from the Stennis stones and leapt downward to the holm where his beloved had lain that weary while. Then he saw that the fair velvet skin was still there, and presently he saw that within the skin his beloved still reposed. He called to her, but she made no answer; with exceeding haste he kneeled down and did off the fair velvet skin, and folded his beloved to his breast. The sun shone full upon her glorious face and kissed away the dew that clung to her white cheeks.

"Thou art redeemed, O my beloved!" cried Harold; but her lips spake not, and her eyes opened not upon him. Yet on the dead wife's face was such a smile as angels wear, and it told him that they should meet again in a love that knoweth no fear of parting. And as Harold held her to his bosom and wailed, there fell down from her hand what she had kept with her to the last, and it lay upon the fair green holm—the little alabaster cross which she had snatched from Theodoric's neck that day the Death-Angel bore the child away.

It was to tell of Harold, the son of Egbert, the son of Ib, and of Persis, his wife, daughter of the Pagan king; and it hath been told. And there is no more to tell, for the tale is ended.

FLAIL, TRASK, AND BISLAND

My quondam friends, Flail, Trask, and Bisland, are no more; they are dead, and with them has gone out of existence as gross an imposition as the moral cowardice of man were capable of inventing, constructing, and practising.

When Alice became my wife she knew that I was a lover and collector of books, but, being a young thing, she had no idea of the monstrous proportions which bibliomania, unchecked, is almost certain to acquire. Indeed, the dear girl innocently and rapturously encouraged this insidious vice. "Some time," she used to say, "we shall have a house of our own, and then your library shall cover the whole top-floor, and the book-cases shall be built in the walls, and there shall be a lovely blue-glass sky-light," etc. Moreover, although she could not tell the difference between an Elzevir and a Pickering, or between a folio and an octavo, Alice was very proud of our little library, and I recall now with real delight the times I used to hear her showing off those precious books to her lady callers. Alice made up for certain inaccuracies of information with a distinct enthusiasm and garrulity that never failed to impress her callers deeply. I was mighty proud of Alice; I was prepared to say, paraphrasing Sam Johnson's remark about the Scotchman, "A wife can be made much of, if caught young."

It was not until after little Grolier and little Richard de Bury were born to us that Alice's regard for my pretty library seemed to abate. I then began to realize the truth of what my bachelor friend Kinzie had often declared—namely, that the chief objection to children was that they weaned the collector from his love of books. Grolier was a mischievous boy, and I had hard work trying to convince his mother that he should by no means be allowed to have his sweet but destructive will with my Bewicks and Bedfords. Thumb and finger marks look well enough in certain places, but I protested that they did not enhance the quaint beauty of an old wood-cut, a delicate binding, or a wide margin. And Richard de Bury—a lovely little 16mo of a child—was almost as destructive as his older brother. The most painful feature of it all to me then was that their mother actually protected the toddling knaves in their vandalism. I never saw another woman change so as Alice did after those two boys came to us. Why, she even suggested to me one day that when we did build our new house we should devote the upper story thereof not to library but to nursery purposes!

Things gradually got to the pass that I began to be afraid to bring books into the house. At first Alice used to reproach me indirectly by eying the new book jealously, and hinting in a subtle, womanly way that Grolier needed new shoes, or that Richard was sadly in need of a new cap. Presently, encouraged by my lamb-like reticence, Alice began to complain gently of what she termed my extravagance, and finally she fell into the pernicious practice of berating me roundly for neglecting my family for the selfish—yes, the cruel—gratification of a foolish fad, and then she would weep and gather up the two boys and wonder how soon we should all be in the poorhouse.

I have spoken of my bachelor friend, Kinzie; there was a philosopher for you, and his philosophy was all the sweeter because it had never been embittered by marital experience. I had confidence in Kinzie, and I told him all about the dilemma I was in. He pitied me and condoled with me, for he was a sympathetic man, and he was, too, as consistent a bibliomaniac as I ever met with. "Be of good cheer," said he, "we shall find a way out of all this trouble." And he suggested a way. I seized upon it as the proverbial drowning man is supposed to clutch at the proverbial straw.

The next time I took a bundle of books home I marched into the house boldly with them. Alice fetched a deep sigh. "Ah, been buying more books, have you?" she asked in a despairing tone.

"No, indeed," I answered triumphantly, "they were given to me—a present from judge Trask. I'm in great luck, ain't I?"

Alice was almost as pleased as I was. The interest with which she inspected the lovely volumes was not feigned. "But who is Judge Trask?" she asked, as she read the autographic lines upon a flyleaf in each book. I explained glibly that the judge was a wealthy and cultured citizen who felt somewhat under obligation to me for certain little services I had rendered him one time and another. I was not to be trapped or cornered. I had learned my sinful lesson perfectly. Alice never so much as suspected me of evil.

The scheme worked so well that I pursued it with more or less diligence. I should say that about twice a week on an average a bundle of books came to the house "with the compliments" of either Judge Trask or Colonel Flail or Mr. Bisland. You can understand that I could not hope to play the Trask deception exclusively and successfully. I invented Colonel Flail and Mr. Bisland, and I contrived to render them quite as liberal in their patronage as the mythical Judge Trask himself. Occasionally a donation came in, by way of variety, from Smeaton and Holbrook and Caswell and other solitary creations of my mendacious imagination, when I used to blind poor dear Alice to the hideous truth.

Touching myself, I gave it out that I had abandoned book-buying, was convinced of the folly of the mania, had reformed, and was repentant. Alice loved me all the better for that, and she became once more the sweetest, most amiable little woman in all the world. She was inexpressibly happy in the fond delusion that I had become prudent and thrifty, and was putting money in bank for that home we were going to buy—sometime.

Meanwhile the names of Flail, Trask, and Bisland became household words with us. Occasionally Smeaton and Holbrook and Caswell were mentioned gratefully as some fair volume bearing their autograph was inspected; but, after all, Flail, Trask, and Bisland were the favorites, for it was from them that most of my beloved books came. Yes, Alice gradually grew to love those three myths; she loved them because they were good to me.

Alice had, like most others of her sex, a strong sense of duty. She determined to do something for my noble friends, and finally she planned a lovely little dinner whereat Judge Trask and Colonel Flail and Mr. Bisland were to be regaled with choicest viands of Alice's choice larder and with the sweetest speeches of Alice's graceful heart. I was authorized only to convey the invitations to this delectable banquet, and here was a pretty plight for a man to be in, surely enough! But my bachelor friend Kinzie (ough, the Mephisto!) helped me out. I reported back to Alice that Judge Trask was out of town, that Colonel Flail was sick abed with grip, and that Mr. Bisland was altogether too shy a man to think of venturing out to a dinner alone. Alice was dreadfully disappointed. Still there was consolation in feeling that she had done her duty in trying to do it.

Well, this system of deception and perjury went on a long time, Alice never suspecting any evil, but perfectly happy in my supposed reform and economy, and in the gracious liberality of those three Maecenas-like friends, Flail, Trask, and Bisland, who kept pouring in rare and beauteous old tomes upon me. She was joyous, too, in the prospect of that new house which we would soon be able to build, now that I had so long quit the old ruinous mania for book-buying! And I—wretch that I was—I humored her in this conceit; I heaped perjury upon perjury; lying and deception had become my second nature. Yet I loathed myself and I hated those books; they reproached me every time I came into their presence. So I was miserable and helpless; how hard it is to turn about when one once gets into the downward path! The shifts I was put to, and the desperate devices which I was forced to employ—I shudder to recall them! Life became a constant, terrifying lie.

Thank Heaven, it is over now, and my face is turned the right way. A third little son was born to us. Alice was, oh! so very ill. When she was convalescing she said to me one day: "Hiram, I have been thinking it all over, and I've made up my mind that we must name the baby Trask Flail Bisland, after our three good friends."

I did n't make any answer, went out into the hall, and communed awhile with my own hideous, tormented self. How my soul revolted against the prospect of giving to that innocent babe a name that would serve simply to scourge me through the rest of my wicked life! No, I could not consent to that. I would be a coward no longer!

I went back into Alice's room, and sat upon the bed beside her, and took one of Alice's dear little white hands in mine, and told her everything, told Alice the whole truth—all about my wickedness and perjuries and deceptions; told her what a selfish, cruel monster I had been; dispelled all the sinful delusion about Flail, Trask, and Bisland; threw myself, penitent and hopeless, upon my deceived, outraged little wife's mercy. Was it a mean advantage to take of a sick woman?

I fancied she would reproach me, for I knew that her heart was set upon that new house she had talked of so often; I told her that the savings she had supposed were in bank, were in reality represented only by and in those stately folios and sumptuous quartos which the mythical Flail, Trask, and Bisland had presumably donated. "But," I added, "I shall sell them now, and with the money I shall build the home in which we may be happy again—a lovely home, sweetheart, with no library at all, but all nursery if you wish it so!"

"No," said Alice, when I had ended my blubbering confession, "we shall not part with the books; they have caused you more suffering than they have me, and, moreover, their presence will have a beneficial effect upon you. Furthermore, I myself have become attached to them—you know I thought they were given to you, and so I have learned to care for them. Poor Judge Trask and Colonel Flail and Mr. Bisland—so they are only myths? Dear Hiram," she added with a sigh, "I can forgive you for everything except for taking those three good men out of our lives!"

After all this I have indeed reformed. I have actually become prudent, and I have a bank-account that is constantly increasing. I do not hate books; I simply do not buy them. And I eschew that old sinner, Kinzie, and all the sinister influences he represents. As for our third little boy, we have named him Reform Meigs, after Alice's mother's grandfather, who built the first saw-mill in what is now the State of Ohio, and was killed by the Indians in 1796.

THE TOUCH IN THE HEART

Old Abel Dunklee was delighted, and so was old Abel's wife, when little Abel came. For this coming they had waited many years. God had prospered them elsewise; this one supreme blessing only had been withheld. Yet Abel had never despaired. "I shall some time have a son," said he. "I shall call him Abel. He shall be rich; he shall succeed to my business; my house, my factory, my lands, my fortune—all shall be his!" Abel Dunklee felt this to be a certainty, and with this prospect constantly in mind he slaved and pinched and bargained. So when at last the little one did come it was as heir to a considerable property.

The joy in the house of Dunklee was not shared by the community at large. Abel Dunklee was by no means a popular man. Folk had the well-defined opinion that he was selfish, miserly, and hard. If he had not been actually bad, he had never been what the world calls a good man. His methods had been of the grinding, sordid order. He had always been scrupulously honest in the payment of his debts, and in keeping his word; but his sense of duty seemed to stop there: Abel's idea of goodness was to owe no man any money. He never gave a penny to charities, and he never spent any time sympathizing with the misfortunes or distresses of other people. He was narrow, close, selfish, and hard, so his neighbors and the community at large said, and I shall not deny that the verdict was a just one.

When a little one comes into this world of ours, it is the impulse of the people here to bid it welcome, and to make its lot pleasant. When little Abel was born no such enthusiasm obtained outside the austere Dunklee household. Popular sentiment found vent in an expression of the hope that the son and heir would grow up to scatter the dollars which old man Dunklee had accumulated by years of relentless avarice and unflagging toil. But Dr. Hardy—he who had officiated in an all-important capacity upon that momentous occasion in the Dunklee household—Dr. Hardy shook his head wisely, and perhaps sadly, as if he were saying to himself: "No, the child will never do either what the old folk or what the other folk would have him do; he is not long for here."

Had you questioned him closely, Dr. Hardy would have told you that little Abel was as frail a babe as ever did battle for life. Dr. Hardy would surely never have dared say that to old Dunklee; for in his rapture in the coming of that little boy old Dunklee would have smote the offender who presumed even to intimate that the babe was not the most vigorous as well as the most beautiful creature upon earth. The old man was simply assotted upon the child—in a selfish way, undoubtedly, but even this selfish love of that puny little child showed that the old man was capable of somewhat better than his past life had been. To hear him talk you might have fancied that Mrs. Dunklee had no part or parcel or interest in their offspring. It was always "my little boy,"—yes, old Abel Dunklee's money had a rival in the old man's heart at last, and that rival was a helpless, shrunken, sickly little babe.

Among his business associates Abel Dunklee was familiarly known as Old Growly, for the reason that his voice was harsh and discordant, and sounded for all the world like the hoarse growling of an ill-natured bear. Abel was not a particularly irritable person, but his slavish devotion to money-getting, his indifference to the amenities of life, his entire neglect of the tender practices of humanity, his rough, unkempt personality, and his deep, hoarse voice—these things combined to make that sobriquet of "Old Growly" an exceedingly appropriate one. And presumably Abel never thought of resenting the slur implied therein and thereby; he was too shrewd not to see that, however disrespectful and evil-intentioned the phrase might be, it served him to good purpose; for it conduced to that very general awe, not to say terror, which kept people from bothering him with their charitable and sentimental schemes.

Yes, I think we can accept it as a fact that Abel liked that sobriquet; it meant more money in his pocket, and fewer demands upon his time and patience.

But Old Growly abroad and Old Growly at home were two very different people. Only the voice was the same. The homely, furrowed, wizened face lighted up, and the keen, restless eyes lost their expression of shrewdness, and the thin, bony hands that elsewhere clutched and clutched and pinched and pinched for possession unlimbered themselves in the presence of little Abel, and reached out their long fingers yearningly and caressingly toward the little child. Then the hoarse voice would growl a salutation that was full of tenderness, for it came straight from the old man's heart; only, had you not known how much he loved the child, you might have thought otherwise, for the old man's voice was always hoarse and discordant, and that was why they called him Old Growly. But what proved his love for that puny babe was the fact that every afternoon, when he came home from the factory, Old Growly brought his little boy a dime; and once, when the little fellow had a fever on him from teething, Old Growly brought him a dollar! Next day the tooth came through and the fever left him, but you could not make the old man believe but what it was the dollar that did it all. That was natural, perhaps; for his life had been spent in grubbing for money, and he had not the soul to see that the best and sweetest things in human life are not to be had by riches alone.

As the doctor had in one way and another intimated would be the case, the child did not wax fat and vigorous. Although Old Growly did not seem to see the truth, little Abel grew older only to become what the doctor had foretold—a cripple. A weakness of the spine was developed, a malady that dwarfed the child's physical growth, giving to his wee face a pinched, starved look, warping his emaciated body, and enfeebling his puny limbs, while at the same time it quickened the intellectual faculties to the degree of precocity. And so two and three and four years went by, little Abel clinging to life with pathetic heroism, and Old Growly loving that little cripple with all the violence of his selfish nature. Never once did it occur to the father that his child might die, that death's seal was already set upon the misshapen little body; on the contrary, Old Growly's thoughts were constantly of little Abel's famous future, of the great fortune he was to fall heir to, of the prosperous business career he was to pursue, of the influence he was to wield in the world—of dollars, dollars, dollars, millions of them which little Abel was some time to possess; these were Old Growly's dreams, and he loved to dream them!

Meanwhile the world did well by the old man; despising him, undoubtedly, for his avarice and selfishness, but constantly pouring wealth, and more wealth, and even more wealth into his coffers. As for the old man, he cared not for what the world thought or said, so long as it paid tribute to him; he wrought on as of old, industriously, shrewdly, hardly, but with this new purpose: to make his little boy happy and great with riches.

Toys and picture-books were vanities in which Old Growly never indulged; to have expended a farthing for chattels of that character would have seemed to Old Growly like sinful extravagance. The few playthings which little Abel had were such as his mother surreptitiously bought; the old man believed that a child should be imbued with a proper regard for the value of money from the very start, so his presents were always cash in hand, and he bought a large tin bank for little Abel, and taught the child how to put the copper and silver pieces into it, and he labored diligently to impress upon the child of how great benefit that same money would be to him by and by. Just picture to yourself, if you can, that fond, foolish old man seeking to teach this lesson to that wan-eyed, pinched-face little cripple! But little Abel took it all very seriously, and was so apt a pupil that Old Growly made great joy and was wont to rub his bony hands gleefully and say to himself, "He has great genius—this boy of mine—great genius for finance!"

But on a day, coming from his factory, Old Growly was stricken with horror to find that during his absence from home a great change had come upon his child. The doctor said it was simply the progress of the disease; that it was a marvel that little Abel had already held out so long; that from the moment of his birth the seal of death had been set upon him in that cruel malady which had drawn his face and warped his body and limbs. Then all at once Old Growly's eyes seemed to be opened to the truth, and like a lightning flash it came to him that perhaps his pleasant dreams which he had dreamed of his child's future could never be realized. It was a bitter awakening, yet amid it all the old man was full of hope, determination, and battle. He had little faith in drugs and nursing and professional skill; he remembered that upon previous occasions cures had been wrought by means of money; teeth had been brought through, the pangs of colic beguiled, and numerous other ailments to which infancy is heir had by the same specific been baffled. So now Old Growly set about wooing his little boy from the embrace of death—sought to coax him back to health with money, and the dimes became dollars, and the tin bank was like to burst of fulness. But little Abel drooped and drooped, and he lost all interest in other things, and he was content to lie, drooping-eyed and listless, in his mother's arms all day. At last the little flame went out with hardly so much as a flutter, and the hope of the house of Dunklee was dissipated forever. But even in those last moments of the little cripple's suffering the father struggled to call back the old look into the fading eyes, and the old smile into the dear, white face. He brought treasure from his vaults and held it up before those fading eyes, and promised it all, all, all—everything he possessed, gold, houses, lands—all he had he would give to that little child if that little child would only live. But the fading eyes saw other things, and the ears that were deaf to the old man's lamentations heard voices that soothed the anguish of that last solemn hour. And so little Abel knew the Mystery.

Then the old man crept away from that vestige of his love, and stood alone in the night, and lifted up his face, and beat his bosom, and moaned at the stars, asking over and over again why he had been so bereaved. And while he agonized in this wise and cried there came to him a voice—a voice so small that none else could hear, a voice seemingly from God; for from infinite space beyond those stars it sped its instantaneous way to the old man's soul and lodged there.

"Abel, I have touched thy heart!"

And so, having come into the darkness of night, old Dunklee went back into the light of day and found life beautiful; for the touch was in his heart.

After that, Old Growly's way of dealing with the world changed. He had always been an honest man, honest as the world goes. But now he was somewhat better than honest; he was kind, considerate, merciful. People saw and felt the change, and they knew why it was so. But the pathetic part of it all was that Old Growly would never admit—no, not even to himself—that he was the least changed from his old grinding, hard self. The good deeds he did were not his own; they were his little boy's—at least so he said. And it was his whim when doing some kind and tender thing to lay it to little Abel, of whom he always spoke as if he were still living. His workmen, his neighbors, his townsmen—all alike felt the graciousness of the wondrous change, and many, ah! many a lowly sufferer blessed that broken old man for succor in little Abel's name. And the old man was indeed much broken: not that he had parted with his shrewdness and acumen, for, as of old, his every venture prospered; but in this particular his mind seemed weakened; that, as I have said, he fancied his child lived, that he was given to low muttering and incoherent mumblings, of which the burden seemed to be that child of his, and that his greatest pleasure appeared now to be watching other little ones at their play. In fact, so changed was he from the Old Growly of former years, that, whereas he had then been wholly indifferent to the presence of those little ones upon earth, he now sought their company, and delighted to view their innocent and mirthful play. And so, presently, the children, from regarding him at first with distrust, came to confide in and love him, and in due time the old man was known far and wide as Old Grampa Growly, and he was pleased thereat. It was his wont to go every fair day, of an afternoon, into a park hard by his dwelling, and mingle with the crowd of little folk there; and when they were weary of their sports they used to gather about him—some even clambering upon his knees—and hear him tell his story, for he had only one story to tell, and that was the story that lay next his heart—the story ever and forever beginning with, "Once ther' wuz a littl' boy." A very tender little story it was, too, told very much more sweetly than I could ever tell it; for it was of Old Grampa Growly's own little boy, and it came from that heart in which the touch—the touch of God Himself—lay like a priceless pearl.

So you must know that the last years of the old man's life made full atonement for those that had gone before. People forgot that the old man had ever been other than he was now, and of course the children never knew otherwise. But as for himself, Old Grampa Growly grew tenderer and tenderer, and his goodness became a household word, and he was beloved of all. And to the very last he loved the little ones, and shared their pleasures, and sympathized with them in their griefs, but always repeating that same old story, beginning with "Once ther' wuz a littl' boy."

The curious part of it was this: that while he implied by his confidences to the children that his own little boy was dead, he never made that admission to others. On the contrary, it was his wont, as I have said, to speak of little Abel as if that child still lived, and, humoring him in this conceit, it was the custom of the older ones to speak always of that child as if he lived and were known and beloved of all. In this custom the old man had great content and solace. For it was his wish that all he gave to and did for charity's sake should be known to come, not from him, but from Abel, his son, and this was his express stipulation at all such times. I know whereof I speak, for I was one of those to whom the old man came upon a time and said: "My little boy—Abel, you know—will give me no peace till I do what he requires. He has this sum of money which he has saved in his bank, count it yourselves, it is $50,000, and he bids me give it to the townsfolk for a hospital, one for little lame boys and girls. And I have promised him—my little boy, Abel, you know—that I will give $50,000 more. You shall have it when that hospital is built." Surely enough, in eighteen months' time the old man handed us the rest of the money, and when we told him that the place was to be called the Abel Dunklee hospital he was sorely distressed, and shook his head, and said: "No, no—not my name! Call it the Little Abel hospital, for little Abel—my boy, you know—has done it all."

The old man lived many years—lived to hear tender voices bless him, and to see pale faces brighten at the sound of his footfall. Yes, for many years the quaint, shuffling figure moved about our streets, and his hoarse but kindly voice—oh, very kindly now!—was heard repeating to the children that pathetic old story of "Once ther' wuz a littl' boy." And where the dear old feet trod the grass grew greenest, and the sunbeams nestled. But at last there came a summons for the old man—a summons from away off yonder—and the old man heard it and went thither.

The doctor—himself hoary and stooping now—told me that toward the last Old Grampa Growly sunk into a sort of sleep, or stupor, from which they could not rouse him. For many hours he lay like one dead, but his thin, creased face was very peaceful, and there was no pain. Children tiptoed in with flowers, and some cried bitterly, while others—those who were younger—whispered to one another: "Hush, let us make no noise; Old Grampa Growly is sleeping."

At last the old man roused up. He had lain like one dead for many hours, but now at last he seemed to wake of a sudden, and, seeing children about him, perhaps he fancied himself in that pleasant park, under the trees, where so very often he had told his one pathetic story to those little ones. Leastwise he made a feeble motion as if he would have them gather nearer, and, seeming to know his wish, the children came closer to him. Those who were nearest heard him say with the ineffable tenderness of old, "Once ther' wuz a littl' boy—"

And with those last sweet words upon his lips, and with the touch in his heart, the old man went down into the Valley.

DANIEL AND THE DEVIL

Daniel was a very wretched man. As he sat with his head bowed upon his desk that evening he made up his mind that his life had been a failure. "I have labored long and diligently," said he to himself, "and although I am known throughout the city as an industrious and shrewd business man, I am still a poor man, and shall probably continue so to the end of my days unless—unless—"

Here Daniel stopped and shivered. For a week or more he had been brooding over his unhappy lot. There seemed to be but one way out of his trouble, yet his soul revolted from taking that step. That was why he stopped and shivered.

"But," he argued, "I must do something! My nine children are growing up into big boys and girls. They must have those advantages which my limited means will not admit of! All my life so far has been pure, circumspect, and rigid; poverty has at last broken my spirit. I give up the fight—I am ready to sell my soul to the Devil!"

"The determination is a wise one," said a voice at Daniel's elbow. Daniel looked up and beheld a grim-visaged stranger in the chair beside him. The stranger was arrayed all in black, and he exhaled a distinct odor of sulphur.

"Am I to understand," asked the stranger, "that you are prepared to enter into a league with the Devil?"

"Yes," said Daniel, firmly; and he set his teeth together after the fashion of a man who is not to be moved from his purpose.

"Then I am ready to treat with you," said the stranger.

"Are you the Devil?" asked Daniel, eying the stranger critically.

"No, but I am authorized to enter into contracts for him," explained the stranger. "My name is Beelzebub, and I am my master's most trusted agent."

"Sir," said Daniel, "you must pardon me (for I am loath to wound your feelings), but one of the rules governing my career as a business man has been to deal directly with principals, and never to trust to the offices of middle-men. The affair now in hand is one concerning the Devil and myself, and between us two and by us two only can the preliminaries be adjusted."

"As it so happens," explained Beelzebub, "this is Friday—commonly called hangman's day—and that is as busy a time in our particular locality as a Monday is in a laundry, or as the first of every month is at a book-keeper's desk. You can understand, perhaps, that this is the Devil's busy day; therefore be content to make this deal with me, and you will find that my master will cheerfully accept any contract I may enter into as his agent and in his behalf."

But no—Daniel would not agree to this; with the Devil himself, and only the Devil himself, would he treat. So he bade Beelzebub go to the Devil and make known his wishes. Beelzebub departed, much chagrined. Presently back came the Devil, and surely it was the Devil this time—there could be no mistake about it; for he wore a scarlet cloak, and had cloven feet, and carried about with him as many suffocating smells as there are kinds of brimstone, sulphur, and assafoetida.

The two talked over all Daniel's miseries; the Devil sympathized with Daniel, and ever and anon a malodorous, gummy tear would trickle down the Devil's sinister nose and drop off on the carpet.

"What you want is money," said the Devil. "That will give you the comfort and the contentment you crave."

"Yes," said Daniel; "it will give me every opportunity to do good."

"To do good!" repeated the Devil. "To do good, indeed! Yes, it's many a good time we shall have together, friend Daniel! Ha, ha, ha!" And the Devil laughed uproariously. Nothing seemed more humorous than the prospect of "doing good" with the Devil's money! But Daniel failed to see what the Devil was so jolly about. Daniel was not a humorist; he was, as we have indicated, a plain business man.

It was finally agreed that Daniel should sell his soul to the Devil upon condition that for the space of twenty-four years the Devil should serve Daniel faithfully, should provide him with riches, and should do whatsoever he was commanded to do; then, at the end of the twenty-fourth year, Daniel's soul was to pass into the possession of the Devil, and was to remain there forever, without recourse or benefit of clergy. Surely a more horrible contract was never entered into!

"You will have to sign your name to this contract," said the Devil, producing a sheet of asbestos paper upon which all the terms of the diabolical treaty were set forth exactly.

"Certainly," replied Daniel. "I have been a business man long enough to know the propriety and necessity of written contracts. And as for you, you must of course give a bond for the faithful execution of your part of this business."

"That is something I have never done before," suggested the Devil.

"I shall insist upon it," said Daniel, firmly. "This is no affair of sentiment; it is strictly and coldly business: you are to do certain service, and are to receive certain rewards therefor—"

"Yes, your soul!" cried the Devil, gleefully rubbing his callous hands together. "Your soul in twenty-four years!"

"Yes," said Daniel. "Now, no contract is good unless there is a quid pro quo."

"That's so," said the Devil, "so let's get a lawyer to draw up the paper for me to sign."

"Why a lawyer?" queried Daniel. "A contract is a simple instrument; I, as a business man, can frame one sufficiently binding."

"But I prefer to have a lawyer do it," urged the Devil.

"And I prefer to do it myself," said Daniel.

When a business man once gets his mind set, not even an Archimedean lever could stir it. So Daniel drew up the bond for the Devil to sign, and this bond specified that in case the Devil failed at any time during the next twenty-four years to do whatso Daniel commanded him, then should the bond which the Devil held against Daniel become null and void, and upon that same day should a thousand and one souls be released forever from the Devil's dominion. The Devil winced; he hated to sign this agreement, but he had to. An awful clap of thunder ratified the abominable treaty, and every black cat within a radius of a hundred leagues straightway fell to frothing and to yowling grotesquely.

Presently Daniel began to prosper; the Devil was a faithful slave, and he served Daniel so artfully that no person on earth suspected that Daniel had leagued with the evil one. Daniel had the finest house in the city, his wife dressed magnificently, and his children enjoyed every luxury wealth could provide. Still, Daniel was content to be known as a business man; he deported himself modestly and kindly; he pursued with all his old-time diligence the trade which in earlier days he had found so unproductive of riches. His indifference to the pleasures which money put within his reach was passing strange, and it caused the Devil vast uneasiness.

"Daniel," said the Devil, one day, "you're not getting out of this thing all the fun there is in it. You go poking along in the same old rut with never a suspicion that you have it in your power to enjoy every pleasure of human life. Why don't you break away from the old restraints? Why don't you avail yourself of the advantages at your command?"

"I know what you 're driving at," said Daniel, shrewdly, "Politics!"

"No, not at all," remonstrated the Devil. "What I mean is fun—gayety. Why not have a good time, Daniel?"

"But I am having a good time," said Daniel. "My business is going along all right, I am rich. I 've got a lovely home; my wife is happy; my children are healthy and contented; I am respected—what more could I ask? What better time could I demand?"

"You don't understand me," explained the Devil. "What I mean by a good time is that which makes the heart merry and keeps the soul youthful and buoyant—wine, Daniel! Wine and the theatre and pretty girls and fast horses and all that sort of happy, joyful life!"

"Tut, tut, tut!" cried Daniel; "no more of that, sir! I sowed my wild oats in college. What right have I to think of such silly follies—I, at forty years of age, and a business man too?"

So not even the Devil himself could persuade Daniel into a life of dissipation. All you who have made a study of the business man will agree that of all human beings he is the hardest to swerve from conservative methods. The Devil groaned and began to wonder why he had ever tied up to a man like Daniel—a business man.

Pretty soon Daniel developed an ambition. He wanted reputation, and he told the Devil so. The Devil's eyes sparkled. "At last," murmured the Devil, with a sigh of relief—"at last."

"Yes," said Daniel, "I want to be known far and wide. You must build a church for me."

"What!" shrieked the Devil. And the Devil's tail stiffened up like a sore thumb.

"Yes," said Daniel, calmly; "you must build a church for me, and it must be the largest and the handsomest church in the city. The sittings shall be free, and you shall provide the funds for its support forever."

The Devil frothed at his mouth, and blue fire issued from his ears and nostrils. He was the maddest devil ever seen on earth.

"I won't do it!" roared the Devil. "Do you suppose I'm going to spend my time building churches and stultifying myself just for the sake of gratifying your idle whims? I won't do it—never!"

"Then the bond I gave is null and void," said Daniel.

"Take your old bond," said the Devil, petulantly.

"But the bond you gave is operative," continued Daniel. "So release the thousand and one souls you owe me when you refuse to obey me."

"Oh, Daniel!" whimpered the Devil, "how can you treat me so? Have n't I always been good to you? Have n't I given you riches and prosperity? Does no sentiment of friendship—"

"Hush," said Daniel, interrupting him. "I have already told you a thousand times that our relations were simply those of one business man with another. It now behooves you to fulfil your part of our compact; eventually I shall fulfil mine. Come, now, to business! Will you or will you not keep your word and save your bond?"

The Devil was sorely put to his trumps. But when it came to releasing a thousand and one souls from hell—ah, that staggered him! He had to build the church, and a noble one it was too. Then he endowed the church, and finally he built a parsonage; altogether it was a stupendous work, and Daniel got all the credit for it. The preacher whom Daniel installed in this magnificent temple was severely orthodox, and one of the first things he did was to preach a series of sermons upon the personality of the Devil, wherein he inveighed most bitterly against that person and his work.

By and by Daniel made the Devil endow and build a number of hospitals, charity schools, free baths, libraries, and other institutions of similar character. Then he made him secure the election of honest men to office and of upright judges to the bench. It almost broke the Devil's heart to do it, but the Devil was prepared to do almost anything else than forfeit his bond and give up those one thousand and one souls. By this time Daniel came to be known far and wide for his philanthropy and his piety. This gratified him of course; but most of all he gloried in the circumstance that he was a business man.

"Have you anything for me to do today?" asked the Devil, one morning. He had grown to be a very meek and courteous devil; steady employment in righteous causes had chastened him to a degree and purged away somewhat of the violence of his nature. On this particular morning he looked haggard and ill—yes, and he looked, too, as blue as a whetstone.

"I am not feeling robust," explained the Devil. "To tell the truth, I am somewhat ill."

"I am sorry to hear it," said Daniel; "but as I am not conducting a sanitarium, I can do nothing further than express my regret that you are ailing. Of course our business relations do not contemplate any interchange of sympathies; still I'll go easy with you to-day. You may go up to the house and look after the children; see that they don't smoke cigarettes, or quarrel, or tease the cat, or do anything out of the way."

Now that was fine business for the Devil to be in; but how could the Devil help himself? He was wholly at Daniel's mercy. He went groaning about the humiliating task.

The crash came at last. It was when the Devil informed Daniel one day that he was n't going to work for him any more.

"You have ruined my business," said the Devil, wearily. "A committee of imps waited upon me last night and told me that unless I severed my connection with you a permanent suspension of my interests down yonder would be necessitated. While I have been running around doing your insane errands my personal business has gone to the dogs—I would n't be at all surprised if I were to have to get a new plant altogether. Meanwhile my reputation has suffered; I am no longer respected, and the number of my recruits is daily becoming smaller. I give up—I can make no further sacrifice."

"Then you are prepared to forfeit your bond?" asked Daniel.

"Not by any means," replied the Devil. "I propose to throw the matter into the courts."

"That will hardly be to your interest," said Daniel, "since, as you well know, we have recently elected honest men to the bench, and, as I recollect, most of our judges are members in good standing of the church we built some years ago!"

The Devil howled with rage. Then, presently, he began to whimper.

"For the last time," expostulated Daniel, "let me remind you that sentiment does not enter into this affair at all. We are simply two business parties coöperating in a business scheme. Our respective duties are exactly defined in the bonds we hold. You keep your contract and I'll keep mine. Let me see, I still have a margin of thirteen years."

The Devil groaned and writhed.

"They call me a dude," whimpered the Devil.

"Who do?" asked Daniel.

"Beelzebub and the rest," said the Devil. "I have been trotting around doing pious errands so long that I 've lost all my sulphur-and-brimstone flavor, and now I smell like spikenard and myrrh."

"Pooh!" said Daniel.

"Well, I do," insisted the Devil. "You've humiliated me so that I hain't got any more ambition. Yes, Daniel, you've worked me shamefully hard!"

"Well," said Daniel, "I have a very distinct suspicion that when, thirteen years hence, I fall into your hands I shall not enjoy what might be called a sedentary life."

The Devil plucked up at this suggestion.
"Indeed you shall not," he muttered.
"I'll make it hot for you!"

"But come, we waste time," said Daniel. "I am a man of business, and I cannot fritter away the precious moments parleying with you. I have important work for you. Tomorrow is Sunday; you are to see that all the saloons are kept closed."

"I sha'n't—I won't!" yelled the Devil.

"But you must," said Daniel, firmly.

"Do you really expect me to do that?" roared the Devil. "Do you fancy that I am so arrant a fool as to shut off the very feeders whereby my hungry hell is supplied? That would be suicidal!"

"I don't know anything about that," said Daniel; "I am a business man, and by this business arrangement of ours it is explicitly stipulated—"

"I don't care what the stipulations are!" shrieked the Devil. "I'm through with you, and may I be consumed by my own fires if ever again I have anything to do with a business man!"

The upshot of it all was that the Devil forfeited his bond, and by this act Daniel was released from every obligation unto the Devil, and one thousand and one souls were ransomed from the torture of the infernal fires.

METHUSELAH

The discussion now going on between our clergymen and certain unbelievers touching the question of Cain and his wife will surely result beneficially, for it will set everybody to reading his Bible more diligently. Still, the biography of Cain is one that we could never become particularly interested in; in short, of all the Old Testament characters none other interests us so much as does Methuselah, the man who lived 969 years. Would it be possible to find in all history another life at once so grand and so pathetic? One can get a faint idea of the awful magnitude of Methuselah's career by pausing to recollect that 969 years represent 9.69 centuries, 96 decades, 11,628 months, 50,388 weeks, 353,928 days, 8,494,272 hours, 521,656,320 minutes, and 36,299,879,200 seconds!

How came he to live so long? Ah, that is easily enough explained. He loved life and the world—both were beautiful to him. And one day he spoke his wish in words. "Oh, that I might live a thousand years!" he cried.

Then looking up straightway he beheld an angel, and the angel said: "Wouldst thou live a thousand years?"

And Methuselah answered him, saying: "As the Lord is my God, I would live a thousand years."

"It shall be even so," said the angel; and then the angel departed out of his sight. So Methuselah lived on and on, as the angel had promised.

How sweet a treasure the young Methuselah must have been to his parents and to his doting ancestors; with what tender solicitude must the old folks have watched the child's progress from the innocence of his first to the virility of his later centuries. We can picture the happy reunions of the old Adam family under the domestic vines and fig-trees that bloomed near the Euphrates. When Methuselah was a mere toddler of nineteen years, Adam was still living, and so was his estimable wife; the possibility is that the venerable couple gave young Methuselah a birthday party at which (we can easily imagine) there were present these following, to-wit: Adam, aged 687; Seth, aged 557; Enos, aged 452; Cainan, aged 362; Mahalaleel, aged 292; Jared, aged 227; Enoch, aged 65, and his infant boy Methuselah, aged 19. Here were represented eight direct generations, and there were present, of course, the wives and daughters; so that, on the whole, the gathering must have been as numerous as it was otherwise remarkable. Nowhere in any of the vistas of history, of romance, or of mythology were it possible to find a spectacle more imposing than that of the child Methuselah surrounded by his father Enoch, his grandfather Jared, his great-grandfather Mahalaleel, his great-great-grandfather Cainan, his great-great-great-grandfather Enos, his great-great-great-great-grandfather Seth, and his great-great-great-great-great-grandfather Adam, as well as by his great-great-great-great-great-grandmother Eve, and her feminine posterity for (say) four centuries! How pretty and how kindly dear old grandma Eve must have looked on that gala occasion, attired, as she must have been, in all the quaint simplicity of that primeval period; and how must the dear old soul have fretted through fear that little Methuselah would eat too many papaws, or drink too much goat's milk. It is a marvel, we think, that in spite of the indulgence and the petting in which he was reared, Methuselah grew to be a good, kind man.

Profane historians agree that just about the time he reached the age of ninety-four Methuselah became deeply enamoured of a comely and sprightly damsel named Mizpah—a young thing scarce turned seventy-six. Up to this period of adolescence his cautious father Enoch had kept Methuselah out of all love entanglements, and it is probable that he would not have approved of this affair with Mizpah had not Jared, the boy's grandfather, counselled Enoch to give the boy a chance. But alas and alackaday for the instability of youthful affection! It befell in an evil time that there came over from the land of Nod a frivolous and gorgeously apparelled beau, who, with finely wrought phrases, did so fascinate the giddy Mizpah that incontinently she gave Methuselah the mitten, and went with the dashing young stranger of 102 as his bride.

This shocking blow so grievously affected Methuselah that for some time (that is to say, for a period of ninety-one years) he shunned female society. But having recovered somewhat from the bitterness of that great disappointment received in the callowness of his ninth decade, he finally met and fell in love with Adah, a young woman of 148, and her he married. The issue of this union was a boy whom they named Lamech, and this child from the very hour of his birth gave his father vast worriment, which, considering the disparity in their ages, is indeed most shocking of contemplation. The tableau of a father (aged 187) vainly coddling a colicky babe certainly does not call for our enthusiasm. Yet we presume to say that Methuselah bore his trials meekly, that he cherished and adored the baby, and that he spent weeks and months playing peek-a-boo and ride-a-cock-horse. In all our consideration of Methuselah we must remember that the mere matter of time was of no consequence to him.

Lamech grew to boyhood, involving his father in all those ridiculous complications which parents nowadays do not heed so much, but which must have been of vast annoyance to a man of Methuselah's advanced age and proper notions. Whittling with the old gentleman's razor, hooking off from school, trampling down the neighbors' rowen, tracking mud into the front parlor—these were some of Lamech's idiosyncrasies, and of course they tormented Methuselah, who recalled sadly that boys were no longer what they used to be when he was a boy some centuries previous. But when he got to be 182 years old Lamech had sowed all his wild oats, and it was then he married a clever young girl of 98, who bore him a son whom they called Noah. Now if Methuselah had been worried and plagued by Lamech, he was more than compensated therefor by this baby grandson, whom he found to be, aside from all prejudices, the prettiest and the smartest child he had ever seen. Old father Adam, who was now turned of his ninth century, tottered over to see the baby, and he, too, allowed that it was an uncommonly bright child. And dear old grandma Eve declared that there was an expression about the upper part of the little Noah's face that reminded her very much of the soft-eyed boy she lost 800 years ago. And dear old grandma Eve used to rock little Noah and sing to him, and cry softly to herself all the while.

Now, in good time, Noah grew to lusty youth, and although he was, on the whole, a joy to his grandsire Methuselah, he developed certain traits and predilections that occasioned the old gentleman much uneasiness. At the tender age of 265 Noah exhibited a strange passion for aquatics, and while it was common for other boys of that time to divert themselves with the flocks and herds, with slingshots and spears, with music and dancing, Noah preferred to spend his hours floating toy-ships in the bayous of the Euphrates. Every day he took his little shittim-wood boats down to the water, tied strings to them, and let them float hither and thither on the crystal bosom of the tide. Naturally enough these practices worried the grandfather mightily.

"May not the crocodiles compass him round about?" groaned Methuselah. "May not behemoth prevail against him? Or, verily, it may befall that the waves shall devour him. Woe is me and lamentation unto this household if destruction come to him through the folly of his fathers!"

So Methuselah's age began to be full of care and trouble, and many a time he felt weary of living, and sometimes—yes, sometimes—he wished he were dead. People in those times were not afraid to die; they believed in the second and better life, because God spoke with them and told them it should be.

The last century of this good man's sojourn upon earth was particularly pathetic. His ancestors were all dead; he alone remained the last living reminiscence of a time that but for him would have been forgotten. Deprived of the wise counsels of his great-great-great-great-great-grandfather Adam and of the gentle admonitions of his great-great-great-great-great-grandmother Eve, Methuselah felt not only lonesome but even in danger of wrong-doing, so precious to him had been the teachings of these worthy progenitors. And what particularly disturbed Methuselah were the dreadful changes that had taken place in society since he was a boy. Dress, speech, customs, and morals were all different now from what they used to be.

When Methuselah was a boy—ah, he remembered it well—people went hither and thither clad only in simple fig-leaf garb; and they were content therewith.

When Methuselah was a boy, people spoke a plain, direct language, strong in its truth, its simplicity, and its honest vigor.

When Methuselah was a boy, manners were open and unaffected, and morals were pure and healthy.

But now all these things were changed. An evil called fashion had filled the minds of men and women with vanity. From the sinful land of Nod and from other pagan countries came divers tradesmen with purples and linens and fine feathers, whereby a wicked pride was engendered, and from these sinful countries, too, came frivolous manners that supplanted the guileless etiquette of the past.

Moreover, traffic and intercourse with the subtle heathen had corrupted and perverted the speech of Adam's time: crafty phrases and false rhetorics had crept in, and the grand old Edenic idioms either were fast being debased or had become wholly obsolete. Such new-fangled words as "eftsoon," "albeit," "wench," "soothly," "zounds," "whenas," and "sithence" had stolen into common usage, making more direct and simpler speech a jest and a byword.

Likewise had prudence given way to extravagance, abstemiousness to intemperance, dignity to frivolity, and continence to lust; so that by these evils was Methuselah grievously tormented, and it repented him full sore that he had lived to see such exceeding wickedness upon earth. But in the midst of all these follies did Methuselah maintain an upright and godly life, and continually did he bless God for that he had held him in the path of rectitude.

Now when Methuselah was in the 964th summer of his sojourn he was called upon to mourn the death of his son Lamech, whom an inscrutable Providence had cut off in what in those days was considered the flower of a man's life—namely, the eighth century thereof. Lamech's untimely decease was a severe blow to his doting father, who, forgetting all his son's boyish indiscretions, remembered now only Lamech's good and lovable traits and deeds. It is reasonable to suppose, however, that the old gentleman was somewhat beguiled from his grief by the lively dispositions and playful antics of Lamech's grandsons, Noah's sons, and his own great-grandsons—Shem, Ham, and Japheth—who at this time had attained to the frolicsome ages of ninety-five, ninety-two, and ninety-one, respectively. These boys inherited from their father a violent penchant for aquatics, and scarcely a day passed that they did not paddle around the bayous and sloughs of the Euphrates in their gopher-wood canoes.

"Gran'pa," Noah used to say, "the conduct of those boys causes me constant vexation. I have no time to follow them around, and I am haunted continually by the fear that they will be drowned, or that the crocodiles will get them if they don't watch out!"

But Methuselah would smiling answer: "Possess thy soul in patience and thy bowels in peace; for verily is it not written 'boys will be boys!'"

Now Shem, Ham, and Japheth were very fond of their great-grandpa, and to their credit be it said that next to paddling over the water privileges of the Euphrates they liked nothing better than to sit in the old gentleman's lap, and to hear him talk about old times. Marvellous tales he told them, too; for his career of nine and a half centuries had been well stocked with incident, as one would naturally suppose. Howbeit, the admiration which these callow youths had for Methuselah was not shared by a large majority of the people then on earth. On the contrary, we blush to admit it, Methuselah was held in very trifling esteem by his frivolous fellow-citizens, who habitually referred to him as an "old 'wayback," "a barnacle," an "old fogy," a "mossback," or a "garrulous dotard," and with singular irreverence they took delight in twitting him upon his senility and in pestering him with divers new-fangled notions altogether distasteful, not to say shocking, to a gentleman of his years.

It was perhaps, however, at the old settlers' picnics, which even then were of annual occurrence, that Methuselah most enjoyed himself; for on these occasions he was given the place of prominence and he was deferred to in everything, since he antedated all the others by at least three centuries. The historians and the antiquarians of the time found him of much assistance to them in their labors, since he was always ready to provide them with dates touching incidents of the remote period from which he had come down unscathed. He remembered vividly how, when he was 186 years of age, the Euphrates had frozen over to a depth of seven feet; the 209th winter of his existence he referred to as "the winter of the deep snow;" he remembered that when he was a boy the women had more character than the women of these later years; he had a vivid recollection of the great plague that prevailed in the city of Enoch during his fourth century; he could repeat, word for word, the address of welcome his great-great-great-great-great-grandfather Adam delivered to an excursion party that came over from the land of Nod one time when Methuselah was a mere child of eighty-seven—oh, yes, poor old Methuselah was full of reminiscence, and having crowded an active career into the brief period of 969 years, it can be imagined that ponderous tomes would not hold the tales he told whenever he was encouraged.

One day, however, Methuselah's grandson Noah took the old gentleman aside and confided into his ear-trumpet a very solemn secret which must have grieved the old gentleman immensely, for he gnashed his gums and wrung his thin, bony hands and groaned dolorously.

"The end of all flesh is at hand," said Noah. "The earth is filled with violence through them, and God will destroy them with the earth. I will make an ark of gopher-wood, the length thereof 300 cubits, the breadth of it 50 cubits, and the height of it 30 cubits, and I will pitch it within and without with pitch. Into the ark will I come, and my sons and my wife, and my sons' wives, and certain living beasts shall come, and birds of the air, and we and they shall be saved. Come thou also, for thou art an austere man and a just."

But as Methuselah sate alone upon his couch that night he thought of his life: how sweet it had been—how that, despite the evil now and then, there had been more of happiness than of sorrow in it. He even forgot the wickedness of the world and remembered only its good and its sunshine, its kindness and its love. He blessed God for it all, and he prayed for the death-angel to come to him ere he beheld the destruction of all he so much loved.

Then the angel came and spread his shadow about the old man.

And the angel said: "Thy prayer is heard, and God doth forgive thee the score-and-ten years of the promised span of thy life."

And Methuselah gathered up his feet into the bed, and prattling of the brooks, he fell asleep; and so he slept with his fathers.

FÉLICE AND PETIT-POULAIN

The name was singularly appropriate, for assuredly Félice was the happiest of all four-footed creatures. Her nature was gentle; she was obedient, long-suffering, kind. She had known what it was to toil and to bear burdens; sometimes she had suffered from hunger and from thirst; and before she came into the possession of Jacques she had been beaten, for Pierre, her former owner, was a hard master. But Félice was always a kind, faithful, and gentle creature; presumably that was why they named her that pretty name, Félice. She may not have been happy when Pierre owned and overworked and starved and beat her; that does not concern us now, for herein it is to tell of that time when she belonged to Jacques, and Jacques was a merciful man.

Jacques was a farmer; he lived a short distance from Cinqville, which, as you are probably aware, is a town of considerable importance upon what used to be the boundary line between France and Germany. The country round about is devoted to agriculture. You can fancy that, with its even roads, leafy woods, quiet lanes, velvety paddocks, tall hedges, and bountiful fields, this country was indeed as pleasant a home as Félice—or, for that matter, any other properly minded horse—could hope for. Toward the southern horizon there were hills that looked a grayish blue from a distance; upon these hills were vineyards, and the wine that came therefrom is very famous wine, as your uncle, if he be a club man, will very truly assure you. There was a pretty little river that curled like a silver snake through the fertile meadows, and lost its way among the hills, and there were many tiny brooks that scampered across lots and got tangled up with that pretty little river in most bewildering fashion. So, as you can imagine, this was a fair country, and you do not wonder that, with so merciful a master as Jacques, our friend Félice was happy.

But what perfected her happiness was the coming of her little colt, as cunning and as blithe a creature as ever whisked a tail or galloped on four legs. I do not know why they called him by that name, but Petit-Poulain was what they called him, and that name seemed to please Félice, for when farmer Jacques came thrice a day to the stile and cried, "Petit-Poulain, petit, petit, Petit-Poulain!" the kind old mother would look up fondly, and, with doting eyes, watch her dainty little colt go bounding toward his calling master. And he was indeed a lovely little fellow. The curé, the holy père François, predicted that in due time that colt would make a great name for himself and a great fortune for his owner. The holy père knew whereof he spake, for in his youth he had tasted of the sweets of Parisian life, and upon one memorable occasion had successfully placed ten francs upon the winner of le grand prix. We can suppose that Félice thought well of the holy père. He never came down the road that she did not thrust her nose through the hedge and give a mild whinny of recognition, as if she fain would say: "Pray stop a moment and see Petit-Poulain and his old mother!"

What happy days those were for Félice and her darling colt. With what tenderness they played together in the paddock; or, when the sky was overcast and a storm came on, with what solicitude would the old mother lead the way into the thatched stable, where there was snug protection against the threatening element. There are those who say that none but humankind is immortal— that none but man has a soul. I do not make or believe that claim. There is that within me which tells me that no thing in this world and life of ours which has felt the grace of maternity shall utterly perish. And this I say in all reverence, and with the hope that I offend neither God nor man.

You are to know that old Félice's devotion to Petit-Poulain was human in its tenderness. As readily, as gladly, and as surely as your dear mother would lay down her life for you would old Félice have yielded up her life for her innocent, blithe darling. So old Félice was happy that pleasant time in that fair country, and Petit-Poulain waxed hale and evermore blithe and beautiful.

Happy days, too, were those for that peaceful country and the other dwellers therein. There was no thought of evil there; the seasons were propitious, the vineyards thrived, the crops were bountiful; as far as eye could see all was prosperity and contentment. But one day the holy Father François came hurrying down the road, and it was too evident that he brought evil tidings. Félice thought it very strange that he paid no heed to her when, as was her wont, she thrust her nose through the hedge and gave a mild whinny of welcome. Anon she saw that he talked long and earnestly with her master Jacques, and presently she saw that Jacques went into the cottage and came again therefrom with his wife Justine and kissed her, and then went away with Père François toward the town off yonder. Félice saw that Justine was weeping, and with never a suspicion of impending evil, she wondered why Justine should weep when all was so prosperous and bright and fair and happy about her. Félice saw and wondered, and meanwhile Petit-Poulain scampered gayly about that velvety paddock.

That night the vineyard hills, bathed in the mellow grace of moonlight, saw a sight they had never seen before. From the east an army came riding and marching on—an army of strange, determined men, speaking a language before unheard in that fair country and threatening things of which that peaceful valley had never dreamed. You and I, of course, know that these were the Germans advancing upon France—a nation of immortals eager to destroy the possessions and the human lives of fellow-immortals! But old Félice, hearing the din away off yonder—the unwonted noise of cavalry and infantry advancing with murderous intent—she did not understand it all, she did not even suspect the truth. You cannot wonder, for what should a soulless beast know of the noble, the human privilege of human slaughter? Old Félice heard that strange din, and instinct led her to coax her little colt from the pleasant paddock into that snug and secure retreat, the thatched stable, and there, in the early morning, they found her, Petit-Poulain pulling eagerly at her generous dugs.

Those who came riding up were strangers in those parts; they were ominously accoutred and they spoke words that old Félice had never heard before. Yes, as you have already guessed, they were German cavalry-men. A battle was impending, and they needed more horses.

"Old enough; but in lieu of a better, she will do." That was what they said. They approached her carefully, for they suspected that she might be vicious. Poor old Félice, she had never harmed even the flies that pestered her. "They are going to put me at the plough," she thought. "It is a long time since I did work of any kind—nothing, in fact, since Petit-Poulain was born. Poor Petit-Poulain will miss me; but I will soon return." With these thoughts she turned her head fondly and caressed her pretty colt.

"The colt must be tied in the stall or he will follow her." So said the cavalrymen. They threw a rope about his neck and made him fast in the stable. Petit-Poulain was very much surprised, and he remonstrated vainly with his fierce little heels.

They put a halter upon old Félice. Justine, the farmer's wife, met them in the yard, and reproached them wildly in French. They laughed boisterously, and answered her in German. Then they rode away, leading old Félice, who kept turning her head and whinnying pathetically, for she was thinking of Petit-Poulain.

Of peace I know and can speak—of peace, with its solace of love, plenty, honor, fame, happiness, and its pathetic tragedy of poverty, heartache, disappointment, tears, bereavement. Of war I know nothing, and never shall know; it is not in my heart of for my hand to break that law which God enjoined from Sinai and Christ confirmed in Galilee. I do not know of war, nor can I tell you of that battle which men with immortal souls fought one glorious day in a fertile country with vineyard hills all round about. But when night fell there was desolation everywhere and death. The Eden was a wilderness; the winding river was choked with mangled corpses; shell and shot had mowed down the acres of waving grain, the exuberant orchards, the gardens and the hedgerows; black, charred ruins, gaunt and ghostlike, marked the spots where homes had stood. The vines had been cut and torn away, and the despoiled hills seemed to crouch down like bereaved mothers under the pitiless gaze of the myriad eyes of heaven.

The victors went their way; a greater triumph was in store for them; a mighty capital was to be besieged; more homes were to be desolated—more blood shed, more hearts broken. So the victors went their way, their hands red and their immortal souls elated.

In the early dawn a horse came galloping homeward. It is Félice, old Félice, riderless, splashed with mud, wild-eyed, sore with fatigue! Félice, Félice, what horrors hast thou not seen! If thou couldst speak, if that tongue of thine could be loosed, what would it say of those who, forgetful of their souls, sink lower than the soulless brutes! Better it is thou canst not speak; the anguish in thine eyes, the despair in thy honest heart, the fear, the awful fear in thy mother breast—what tongue could utter them?

Adown the road she galloped—the same road she had traversed, perhaps, a thousand times before, yet it was so changed now she hardly knew it. Twenty-four hours had ruthlessly levelled the noble trees, the hedgerows, and the fields of grain. Twenty-four hours of battle had done all this and more. In all those ghastly hours, one thought had haunted Félice; one thought alone—the thought of Petit-Poulain! She pictured him tied in that far-away stall, wondering why she did not come. He was hungry, she knew; her dugs were full of milk and they pained her; how sweet would be her relief when her Petit-Poulain broke his long fast. Petit-Poulain, Petit-Poulain, Petit-Poulain—this one thought and this alone had old Félice throughout those hours of battle and of horror.

Could this have been the farm-house? It was a ruin now. Shells had torn it apart. Where was the good master Jacques; had he gone with the curé to the defence of the town? And Justine—where was she? Bullets had cut away the rose-trees and the smoke-bush; the garden was no more. The havoc, the desolation, was complete. The cote, which had surmounted the pole around which an ivy twined, had been swept away. The pigeons now circled here and there bewildered; wondering, perhaps, why Justine did not come and call to them and feed them.

To this seared, scarred spot came old Félice. He that had ridden her into battle lay with his face downward near those distant vineyard hills. His blood had stained Félice's neck; a bullet had grazed her flank, but that was a slight wound—riderless, she turned and came from the battle-field and sought her Petit-Poulain once again.

Hard by the ruins of cottage, of garden, and of cote, she came up standing; she was steaming and breathless. She rolled her eyes wildly around—she looked for the stable where she had left Petit-Poulain. She trembled as if an overwhelming apprehension of disaster suddenly possessed her. She gave a whinny, pathetic in its tenderness. She was calling Petit-Poulain. But there was no answer.

Petit-Poulain lay dead in the ruins of the stable. His shelter had not escaped the fury of the battle. He could not run away, for they had tied him fast when they carried his old mother off. So now he lay amid that debris, his eyes half open in death and his legs stretched out stark and stiff.

And old Félice—her udder bursting with the maternal grace he never again should know, and her heart breaking with the agony of sudden and awful bereavement—she staggered, as if blinded by despair, toward that vestige of her love, and bent over him and caressed her Petit-Poulain.

Once upon a time a little boy came, during his play, to the bank of a river. The waters of the river were very dark and wild, and there was so black a cloud over the river that the little boy could not see the further shore. An icy wind came up from the cloud and chilled the little boy, and he trembled with cold and fear as the wind smote his cheeks and ran its slender icicle fingers through his yellow curls. An old man sat on the bank of the river; he was very, very old; his head and shoulders were covered with a black mantle; and his beard was white as snow.

"Will you come with me, little boy?" asked the old man.

"Where?" inquired the little boy.

"To yonder shore," replied the old man.

"Oh, no; not to that dark shore," said the little boy. "I should be afraid to go."

"But think of the sunlight always there," said the old man, "the birds and flowers; and remember there is no pain, nor anything of that kind to vex you."

The little boy looked and saw the dark cloud hanging over the waters, and he felt the cold wind come up from the river; moreover, the sight of the strange man terrified him. So, hearing his mother calling him, the little boy ran back to his home, leaving the old man by the river alone.

Many years after that time the little boy came again to the river; but he was not a little boy now—he was a big, strong man.

"The river is the same," said he; "the wind is the same cold, cutting wind of ice, and the same black cloud obscures yonder shore. I wonder where the strange old man can be."

"I am he," said a solemn voice.

The man turned and looked on him who spoke, and he saw a warrior clad in black armor and wielding an iron sword.

"No, you are not he!" cried the man. "You are a warrior come to do me harm."

"I am indeed a warrior," said the other. "Come with me across the river."

"No," replied the man, "I will not go with you. Hark, I hear the voices of my wife and children calling to me—I will return to them!"

The warrior strove to hold him fast and bear him across the river to the yonder shore, but the man prevailed against him and returned to his wife and little ones, and the warrior was left upon the river-bank.

Then many years went by and the strong man became old and feeble. He found no pleasure in the world, for he was weary of living. His wife and children were dead, and the old man was alone. So one day in those years he came to the bank of the river for the third time, and he saw that the waters had become quiet and that the wind which came up from the river was warm and gentle and smelled of flowers; there was no dark cloud overhanging the yonder shore, but in its place was a golden mist through which the old man could see people walking on the yonder shore and stretching out their hands to him, and he could hear them calling him by name. Then he knew they were the voices of his dear ones.

"I am weary and lonesome," cried the old man. "All have gone before me: father, mother, wife, children—all whom I have loved. I see them and hear them on yonder shore, but who will bear me to them?"

Then a spirit came in answer to this cry. But the spirit was not a strange old man nor yet an armored warrior; but as he came to the river's bank that day he was a gentle angel, clad in white; his face was very beautiful, and there was divine tenderness in his eyes.

"Rest thy head upon my bosom," said the angel, "and I will bear thee across the river to those who call thee."

So, with the sweet peace of a little child sinking to his slumbers, the old man drooped in the arms of the angel and was borne across the river to those who stood upon the yonder shore and called.

FRANZ ABT

Many years ago a young composer was sitting in a garden. All around bloomed beautiful roses, and through the gentle evening air the swallows flitted, twittering cheerily. The young composer neither saw the roses nor heard the evening music of the swallows; his heart was full of sadness and his eyes were bent wearily upon the earth before him.

"Why," said the young composer, with a sigh, "should I be doomed to all this bitter disappointment? Learning seems vain, patience is mocked—fame is as far from me as ever."

The roses heard his complaint. They bent closer to him and whispered, "Listen to us—listen to us." And the swallows heard him, too, and they flitted nearer him; and they, too, twittered, "Listen to us—listen to us." But the young composer was in no mood to be beguiled by the whisperings of the roses and the twitterings of the birds; with a heavy heart and sighing bitterly he arose and went his way.

It came to pass that many times after that the young composer came at evening and sat in the garden where the roses bloomed and the swallows twittered; his heart was always full of disappointment, and often he cried out in anguish against the cruelty of fame that it came not to him. And each time the roses bent closer to him, and the swallows flew lower, and there in the garden the sweet flowers and little birds cried, "Listen to us—listen to us, and we will help you."

And one evening the young composer, hearing their gentle pleadings, smiled sadly, and said: "Yes, I will listen to you. What have you to say, pretty roses?"

"Make your songs of us," whispered the roses—"make your songs of us."

"Ha, ha!" laughed the composer. "A song of the roses would be very strange, indeed! No, sweet flowers—it is fame I seek, and fame would scorn even the beauty of your blushes and the subtlety of your perfumes."

"You are wrong," twittered the swallows, flying lower. "You are wrong, foolish man. Make a song for the heart—make a song of the swallows and the roses, and it will be sung forever, and your fame shall never die."

But the composer laughed louder than before; surely there never had been a stranger suggestion than that of the roses and the swallows! Still, in his chamber that night the composer thought of what the swallows had said, and in his dreams he seemed to hear the soft tones of the roses pleading with him. Yes, many times thereafter the composer recalled what the birds and flowers had said, but he never would ask them as he sat in the garden at evening how he could make the heart-song of which they chattered. And the summer sped swiftly by, and one evening when the composer came into the garden the roses were dead, and their leaves lay scattered on the ground. There were no swallows fluttering in the sky, and the nests under the eaves were deserted. Then the composer knew his little friends were beyond recall, and he was oppressed by a feeling of loneliness. The roses and the swallows had grown to be a solace to the composer, had stolen into his heart all unawares—now that they were gone, he was filled with sadness.

"I will do as they counselled," said he; "I will make a song of them—a song of the swallows and the roses. I will forget my greed for fame while I write in memory of my little friends."

Then the composer made a song of the swallows and the roses, and, while he wrote, it seemed to him that he could hear the twittering of the little birds all around him, and scent the fragrance of the flowers, and his soul was warmed with a warmth he had never felt before, and his tears fell upon his manuscript.

When the world heard the song which the composer had made of the swallows and the roses, it did homage to his genius. Such sentiment, such delicacy, such simplicity, such melody, such heart, such soul—ah, there was no word of rapturous praise too good for the composer now: fame, the sweetest and most enduring kind of fame, had come to him.

And the swallows and the roses had done it all. Their subtle influences had filled the composer's soul with a great inspiration—by means like this God loves to speak to the human heart.

"We told you so," whispered the roses when they came again in the spring. "We told you that if you sang of us the world would love your song."

Then the swallows, flying back from the south, twittered: "We told you so; sing the songs the heart loves, and you shall live forever."

"Ah, dear ones," said the composer, softly; "you spoke the truth. He who seeks a fame that is immortal has only to reach and abide in the human heart."

The lesson he learned of the swallows and the roses he never forgot. It was the inspiration and motive of a long and beautiful life. He left for others that which some called a loftier ambition. He was content to sit among the flowers and hear the twitter of birds and make songs that found an echo in all breasts. Ah, there was such a beautiful simplicity—such a sweet wisdom in his life! And where'er the swallows flew, and where'er the roses bloomed, he was famed and revered and beloved, and his songs were sung.

Then his hair grew white at last, and his eyes were dim and his steps were slow. A mortal illness came upon him, and he knew that death was nigh.

"The winter has been long," said he, wearily. "Open the window and raise me up that I may see the garden, for it must be that spring is come."

It was indeed spring, but the roses had not yet bloomed. The swallows were chattering in their nests under the eaves or flitting in the mild, warm sky.

"Hear them," he said faintly. "How sweetly they sing. But alas! where are the roses?"

Where are the roses? Heaped over thee, dear singing heart; blooming on thy quiet grave in the Fatherland, and clustered and entwined all in and about thy memory, which with thy songs shall go down from heart to heart to immortality.

MISTRESS MERCILESS

This is to tell of our little Mistress Merciless, who for a season abided with us, but is now and forever gone from us unto the far-off land of Ever-Plaisance. The tale is soon told; for it were not seemly to speak all the things that are in one's heart when one hath to say of a much-beloved child, whose life here hath been shortened so that, in God's wisdom and kindness, her life shall be longer in that garden that bloometh far away.

You shall know that all did call her Mistress Merciless; but her mercilessness was of a sweet, persuasive kind: for with the beauty of her face and the music of her voice and the exceeding sweetness of her virtues was she wont to slay all hearts; and this she did unwittingly, for she was a little child. And so it was in love that we did call her Mistress Merciless, just as it was in love that she did lord it over all our hearts.

Upon a time walked she in a full fair garden, and there went with her an handmaiden that we did call in merry wise the Queen of Sheba; for this handmaiden was in sooth no queen at all, but a sorry and ill-favored wench; but she was assotted upon our little Mistress Merciless and served her diligently, and for that good reason was vastly beholden of us all. Yet, in a jest, we called her the Queen of Sheba; and I make a venture that she looked exceeding fair in the eyes of our little Mistress Merciless: for the eyes of children look not upon the faces but into the hearts and souls of others. Whilst these two walked in the full fair garden at that time they came presently unto an arbor wherein there was a rustic seat, which was called the Siege of Restfulness; and hereupon sate a little sick boy that, from his birth, had been lame, so that he could not play and make merry with other children, but was wont to come every day into this full fair garden and content himself with the companionship of the flowers. And, though he was a little lame boy, he never trod upon those flowers; and even had he done so, methinks the pressure of those crippled feet had been a caress, for the little lame boy was filled with the spirit of love and tenderness. As the tiniest, whitest, shrinking flower exhaleth the most precious perfume, so in and from this little lame boy's life there came a grace that was hallowing in its beauty.

Since they never before had seen him, they asked him his name; and he answered them that of those at home he was called Master Sweetheart, a name he could not understand: for surely, being a cripple, he must be a very sorry sweetheart; yet, that he was a sweetheart unto his mother at least he had no doubt, for she did love to hold him in her lap and call him by that name; and many times when she did so he saw that tears were in her eyes—a proof, she told him when he asked, that Master Sweetheart was her sweetheart before all others upon earth.

It befell that our little Mistress Merciless and Master Sweetheart became fast friends, and the Queen of Sheba was handmaiden to them both; for the simple, loyal creature had not a mind above the artless prattle of childhood, and the strange allegory of the lame boy's speech filled her with awe, even as the innocent lisping of our little Mistress Merciless delighted her heart and came within the comprehension of her limited understanding. So each day, when it was fair, these three came into the full fair garden, and rambled there together; and when they were weary they entered into the arbor and sate together upon the Siege of Restfulness. Wit ye well there was not a flower or a tree or a shrub or a bird in all that full fair garden which they did not know and love, and in very sooth every flower and tree and shrub and bird therein did know and love them.

When they entered into the arbor, and sate together upon the Siege of Restfulness, it was Master Sweetheart's wont to tell them of the land of Ever-Plaisance, for it was a conceit of his that he journeyed each day nearer and nearer to that land, and that his journey thitherward was nearly done. How came he to know of that land I cannot say, for I do not know; but I am fain to believe that, as he said, the exceeding fair angels told him thereof when by night, as he lay sleeping, they came singing and with caresses to his bedside.

I speak now of a holy thing, therefore I speak truth when I say that while little children lie sleeping in their beds at night it pleaseth God to send His exceeding fair angels with singing and caresses to bear messages of His love unto those little sleeping children. And I have seen those exceeding fair angels bend with folded wings over the little cradles and the little beds, and kiss those little sleeping children and whisper God's messages of love to them, and I knew that those messages were full of sweet tidings; for, even though they slept, the little children smiled. This have I seen, and there is none who loveth little children that will deny the truth of this thing which I have now solemnly declared.

Of that land of Ever-Plaisance was our little Mistress Merciless ever fain to hear tell. But when she beset the rest of us to speak thereof we knew not what to say other than to confirm such reports as Master Sweetheart had already made. For when it cometh to knowing of that far-off land—ah me, who knoweth more than the veriest little child? And oftentimes within the bosom of a little, helpless, fading one there bloometh a wisdom which sages cannot comprehend. So when she asked us we were wont to bid her go to Master Sweetheart, for he knew the truth and spake it.

It is now to tell of an adventure which on a time befell in that full fair garden of which you have heard me speak. In this garden lived many birds of surpassing beauty and most rapturous song, and among them was one that they called Joyous, for that he did ever carol forth so joyously, it mattered not what the day soever might be. This bird Joyous had his home in the top of an exceeding high tree, hard by the pleasant arbor, and here did he use to sit at such times as the little people came into that arbor, and then would he sing to them such songs as befitted that quiet spot, and them that came thereto. But there was a full evil cat that dwelt near by, and this cruel beast found no pleasure in the music that Joyous did make continually; nay, that music filled this full evil cat with a wicked thirst for the blood of that singing innocent, and she had no peace for the malice that was within her seeking to devise a means whereby she might comprehend the bird Joyous to her murderous intent. Now you must know that it was the wont of our little Mistress Merciless and of Master Sweetheart to feed the birds in that fair garden with such crumbs as they were suffered to bring with them into the arbor, and at such times would those birds fly down with grateful twitterings and eat of those crumbs upon the greensward round about the arbor. Wit ye well, it was a merry sight to see those twittering birds making feast upon the good things which those children brought, and our little Mistress Merciless and little Master Sweetheart had sweet satisfaction therein. But, on a day, whilst thus those twittering birds made great feasting, lo! on a sudden did that full evil cat whereof I have spoken steal softly from a thicket, and with one hideous bound make her way into the very midst of those birds and seize upon that bird Joyous, that was wont to sing so merrily from the tree hard by the arbor. Oh, there was a mighty din and a fearful fluttering, and the rest flew swiftly away, but Joyous could not do so, because the full evil cat held him in her cruel fangs and claws. And I make no doubt that Joyous would speedily have met his death, but that with a wrathful cry did our little Mistress Merciless hasten to his rescue. And our little Mistress belabored that full evil cat with Master Sweetheart's crutch, until that cruel beast let loose her hold upon the fluttering bird and was full glad to escape with her aching bones into the thicket again. So it was that Joyous was recovered from death; but even then might it have fared ill with him, had they not taken him up and dressed his wounds and cared for him until duly he was well again. And then they released him to do his plaisance, and he returned to his home in the tree hard by the arbor and there he sung unto those children more sweetly than ever before; for his heart was full of gratitude to our little Mistress Merciless and Master Sweetheart.

Now, of the dolls that she had in goodly number, that one which was named Beautiful did our little Mistress Merciless love best. Know well that the doll Beautiful had come not from oversea, and was neither of wax nor of china; but she was right ingeniously constructed of a bed-key that was made of wood, and unto the top of this bed-key had the Queen of Sheba superadded a head with a fair face, and upon the body and the arms of the key had she hung passing noble raiment. Unto this doll Beautiful was our little Mistress Merciless vastly beholden, and she did use to have the doll Beautiful lie by her side at night whilst she slept, and whithersoever during the day she went, there also would she take the doll Beautiful, too. Much sorrow and lamentation, therefore, made our little Mistress Merciless when on an evil day the doll Beautiful by chance fell into the fish-pond, and was not rescued therefrom until one of her beauteous eyes had been devoured of the envious water; so that ever thereafter the doll Beautiful had but one eye, and that, forsooth, was grievously faded. And on another evil day came a monster ribald dog pup and seized upon the doll Beautiful whilst she reposed in the arbor, and bore her away, and romped boisterously with her upon the sward, and tore off her black-thread hair, and sought to destroy her wholly, which surely he would have done but for the Queen of Sheba, who made haste to rescue the doll Beautiful, and chastise that monster ribald dog pup.

Therefore, as you can understand, the time was right busily spent. The full fair garden, with its flowers and the singing birds and the gracious arbor and the Siege of Restfulness, found favor with those children, and amid these joyous scenes did Master Sweetheart have to tell each day of that far-off land of Ever-Plaisance, whither he said he was going. And one day, when the sun shone very bright, and the full fair garden joyed in the music of those birds, Master Sweetheart did not come, and they missed the little lame boy and wondered where he was. And as he never came again they thought at last that of a surety he had departed into that country whereof he loved to tell. Which thing filled our little Mistress Merciless with wonder and inquiry; and I think she was lonely ever after that—lonely for Master Sweetheart.

I am thinking now of her and of him; for this is the Christmas season—the time when it is most meet to think of the children and other sweet and holy things. There is snow everywhere, snow and cold. The garden is desolate and voiceless: the flowers are gone, the trees are ghosts, the birds have departed. It is winter out there, and it is winter, too, in this heart of mine. Yet in this Christmas season I think of them, and it pleaseth me—God forbid that I offend with much speaking—it pleaseth me to tell of the little things they did and loved. And you shall understand it all if, perchance, this sacred Christmas time a little Mistress Merciless of your own, or a little Master Sweetheart, clingeth to your knee and sanctifieth your hearthstone.

When of an evening all the joy of day was done, would our little Mistress Merciless fall aweary; and then her eyelids would grow exceeding heavy and her little tired hands were fain to fold. At such a time it was my wont to beguile her weariness with little tales of faery, or with the gentle play that sleepy children like. Much was her fancy taken with what I told her of the train that every night whirleth away to Shut-Eye Town, bearing unto that beauteous country sleepy little girls and boys. Nor would she be content until I told her thereof—yes, every night whilst I robed her in her cap and gown would she demand of me that tale of Shut-Eye Town, and the wonderful train that was to bear her thither. Then would I say in this wise:—

At Bedtime-ville there is a train of cars that waiteth for you, my sweet—for you and for other little ones that would go to quiet, slumbrous Shut-Eye Town.

But make no haste; there is room for all. Each hath a tiny car that is snug and warm, and when the train starteth each car swingeth soothingly this way and that way, this way and that way, through all the journey of the night.

Your little gown is white and soft; your little cap will hold those pretty curls so fast that they cannot get away. Here is a curl that peepeth out to see what is going to happen. Hush, little curl! make no noise; we will let you peep out at the wonderful sights, but you must not tell the others about it; let them sleep, snuggled close together.

The locomotive is ready to start. Can you not hear it?

"Shug-chug! Shug-chug! Shug-chug!" That is what the locomotive is saying, all to itself. It knoweth how pleasant a journey it is about to make.

"Shug-chug! Shug-chug! Shug-chug!"

Oh, many a time hath it proudly swept over prairie and hill, over river and plain, through sleeping gardens and drowsy cities, swiftly and quietly, bearing the little ones to the far, pleasant valley where lieth Shut-Eye Town.

"Shug-chug! Shug-chug! Shug-chug!"

So sayeth the locomotive to itself at the station in Bedtime-ville; for it knoweth how fair and far a journey is before it.

Then a bell soundeth. Surely my little one heareth the bell!

"Ting-long! Ting-a-long! Ting-long!"

So soundeth the bell, and it seemeth to invite you to sleep and dreams.

"Ting-long! Ting-a-long! Ting-long!"

How sweetly ringeth and calleth that bell.

"To sleep—to dreams, O little lambs!" it seemeth to call. "Nestle down close, fold your hands, and shut your dear eyes! We are off and away to Shut-Eye Town! Ting-long! Ting-a-long! Ting-long! To sleep—to dreams, O little cosset lambs!"

And now the conductor calleth out in turn. "All aboard!" he calleth, "All aboard for Shut-Eye Town!" he calleth in a kindly tone.

But, hark ye, dear-my-soul, make thou no haste; there is room for all. Here is a cosey little car for you. How like your cradle it is, for it is snug and warm, and it rocketh this way and that way, this way and that way, all night long, and its pillows caress you tenderly. So step into the pretty nest, and in it speed to Shut-Eye Town.

"Toot! Toot!"

That is the whistle. It soundeth twice, but it must sound again before the train can start. Now you have nestled down, and your dear hands are folded; let your two eyes be folded, too, my sweet; for in a moment you shall be rocked away, and away, away into the golden mists of Balow!

"Ting-long! Ting-a-long! Ting-long!"

"All aboard!"

"Toot! Toot! Toot!"

And so my little golden apple is off and away for Shut-Eye Town!

Slowly moveth the train, yet faster by degrees. Your hands are folded, my beloved, and your dear eyes they are closed; and yet you see the beauteous sights that skirt the journey through the mists of Balow. And it is rockaway, rockaway, rockaway, that your speeding cradle goes—rockaway, rockaway, rockaway, through the golden glories that lie in the path that leadeth to Shut-Eye Town.

"Toot! Toot!"

So crieth the whistle, and it is "down-brakes," for here we are at Ginkville, and every little one knoweth that pleasant waking-place, where mother with her gentle hands holdeth the gracious cup to her sleepy darling's lips.

"Ting-long! Ting-a-long! Ting-long!" and off is the train again. And swifter and swifter it speedeth— oh, I am sure no other train speedeth half so swiftly! The sights my dear one sees! I cannot tell of them—one must see those beauteous sights to know how wonderful they are!

"Shug-chug! Shug-chug! Shug-chug!"

On and on and on the locomotive proudly whirleth the train.

"Ting-long! Ting-a-long! Ting-long!"

The bell calleth anon, but fainter and evermore fainter; and fainter and fainter groweth that other calling—"Toot! Toot! Toot!"—till finally I know that in that Shut-Eye Town afar my dear one dreameth the dreams of Balow.

This was the bedtime tale which I was wont to tell our little Mistress Merciless, and at its end I looked upon her face to see it calm and beautiful in sleep.

Then was I wont to kneel beside her little bed and fold my two hands—thus—and let my heart call to the host invisible: "O guardian angels of this little child, hold her in thy keeping from all the perils of darkness and the night! O sovereign Shepherd, cherish Thy little lamb and mine, and, Holy Mother, fold her to thy bosom and thy love! But give her back to me—when morning cometh, restore ye unto me my little one!"

But once she came not back. She had spoken much of Master Sweetheart and of that land of Ever-Plaisance whither he had gone. And she was not afeared to make the journey alone; so once upon a time when our little Mistress Merciless bade us good-by, and went away forever, we knew that it were better so; for she was lonely here, and without her that far-distant country whither she journeyed were not content. Though our hearts were like to break for love of her, we knew that it were better so.

The tale is told, for it were not seemly to speak all the things that are in one's heart when one hath to say of a much-beloved child whose life here hath been shortened so that, in God's wisdom and kindness, her life shall be longer in that garden that bloometh far away.

About me are scattered the toys she loved, and the doll Beautiful hath come down all battered and grim—yet, oh! so very precious to me, from those distant years; yonder fareth the Queen of Sheba in her service as handmaiden unto me and mine—gaunt and doleful-eyed, yet stanch and sturdy as of old. The garden lieth under the Christmas snow—the garden where ghosts of trees wave their arms and moan over the graves of flowers; the once gracious arbor is crippled now with the infirmities of age, the Siege of Restfulness fast sinketh into decay, and long, oh! long ago did that bird Joyous carol forth his last sweet song in the garden that was once so passing fair.

And amid it all—this heartache and the loneliness which the years have brought—cometh my Christmas gift to-day: the solace of a vision of that country whither she—our little Mistress Merciless—hath gone; a glimpse of that far-off land of Ever-Plaisance.

THE PLATONIC BASSOON

All who knew the beautiful and accomplished Aurora wondered why she did not marry. She had now reached the mature age of twenty-five years, and was in full possession of those charms which are estimated by all men as the choicest gifts a woman can possess. You must know that Aurora had a queenly person, delightful manners, an extensive education, and an amiable disposition; and, being the only child of wealthy parents, she should not have lacked the one thing that seemed necessary to perfect and round out her usefulness as a member of society.

The truth was, Aurora did not fancy the male sex. She regarded men as conveniences that might come handy at times when an escort to the theatre was required, or when a partner in a dance was demanded, when a fan was to be picked up, or when an errand was to be run; but the idea of marrying any man was as distasteful to Aurora as the proposition to marry a hat-rack or any other piece of household furniture would have been.

The secret of this strange aversion might have been traced to Aurora's maiden aunt Eliza, who had directed Aurora's education, and had from her niece's early youth instilled into Aurora's mind very distinct notions touching the masculine sex.

Aurora had numerous admirers among the young gentlemen who moved in the same elevated social circle as herself and frequently called at her father's house. Any one of them would gladly have made her his wife, and many of them had expressed a tender yearning for her life companionship. But Aurora was quick to recognize in each suitor some objectionable trait or habit or feature which her aunt Eliza had told about, and which imperatively prohibited a continuance of the young gentleman's attentions.

Aurora's father could not understand why his daughter was so hypercritical and fastidious in a matter which others of her sex were so apt to accept with charitable eyes. "They are bright, honest fellows," he urged, "worthy of any girl's love. Receive their advances kindly, my child, and having chosen one among them, you will be the happier for it."

"Never mind, Aurora," said Aunt Eliza. "Men are all alike. They show their meanness in different ways, but the same spirit of evil is in 'em all. I have lived in this world forty-six years, and during that time I have found men to be the most unfeeling and most untrustworthy of brutes."

So it was that at the age of twenty-five Aurora was found beautiful, amiable, and accomplished, but thoroughly and hopelessly a man-hater. And it was about this time that she became involved in that unhappy affair which even to this day is talked of by those who knew her then.

On the evening of a certain day Aurora attended the opera with her father and mother and Morgan Magnus, the young banker. Their box at the opera was so close to the orchestra that by reaching out her hand Aurora could have touched several of the instruments. Now it happened that a bassoon was the instrument nearest the box in which Aurora sat, and it was natural therefore that the bassoon attracted more of Aurora's attention than any other instrument in the orchestra. If you have never beheld or heard a bassoon you are to understand that it is an instrument of wood, of considerable more length than breadth, provided with numerous stops and keys, and capable of producing an infinite variety of tones, ranging from the depth of lugubriousness to the highest pitch of vivacity. This particular bassoon was of an appearance that bordered upon the somber, the polished white of his keys emphasizing the solemn black of his long, willowy body. And, as he loomed up above the serene bald head of the musician that played him, Aurora thought she had never seen a more distingué object.

The opera was "Il Trovatore," a work well calculated to call in play all that peculiar pathos of which the bassoon is capable. When Aurora saw the player raise the bassoon and apply the tiny tube thereunto appertaining to his lips, and heard him evoke from the innermost recesses of the bassoon tones that were fairly reeking with tears and redolent of melancholy, she felt a curious sentiment of pity awakened in her bosom.

Aurora had seen many an agonized swain at her feet, and had heard his impassioned pleadings for mercy; she had perused many a love missive wherein her pity was eloquently implored, but never had she experienced the tender, melting sentiment that percolated through her breast when she heard the bassoon mingling his melancholy tones with Manrico's plaints. The tears welled up into Aurora's eyes, her bosom heaved convulsively, and the most subtle emotions thrilled her soul.

In vain did young Magnus, the banker, seek to learn the cause of her agitation, and it seemed like a cruel mockery when Aurora's mother said: "You must remember, dear, that it is not real; it is only a play." After this memorable evening, wherein an unexpected and indescribable sweetness had crept into the young woman's life, Aurora more frequently insisted upon going to the opera. A strange fascination attracted her thither, and on each succeeding evening she found some new beauty in the bassoon, some new phase in his kaleidoscopic character to wonder at, some new accomplishment to admire. On one occasion—it was at the opera bouffe—this musical prodigy exhibited a playfulness and an exuberance of wit and humor that Aurora had never dreamed of. He ran the gamut of vocal conceit, and the polyglot fertility of his fancy simply astounded his rapt auditor. She was dazed, enchanted, spellbound. So here we find the fair Aurora passing from the condition of pity into the estate of admiration.

And now, having first conceived a wondrous pity for the bassoon, and then having become imbued with an admiration of his wit, sarcasm, badinage, repartee, and humor, it followed naturally and logically that Aurora should fall desperately in love with him; for pity and admiration are but the forerunners of the grand passion.

"Aunt Eliza," said Aurora one day, "you have instilled into my sensitive nature an indelible aversion to men, compared with which all such deleble passions as affection and love are as inconsequential as summer zephyrs. I believe men to be by nature and practice gross, vulgar, sensual, and unworthy; and from this opinion I feel that I shall never recede. Yet such a clinging and fragile thing is woman's heart that it must needs have some object about which it may twine, even as the gentle ivy twines about the oak. Now, as you know, some women there are who, convinced of the utter worthlessness of the opposite sex, dedicate their lives to the adoration of some art or science, lavishing thereupon that love which women less prudent squander upon base men and ungrateful children; in the painting of pictures, devotion to the drama, the cultivation of music, pursuit of trade, or the exclusive attention to a profession, some women find the highest pleasure. But you and I, dear aunt, who are directed by even higher and purer motives than these women, scorn the pursuits of the arts and sciences, the professions and trades, and lay our hearts as willing sacrifices upon the altars of a tabby cat and a bassoon. What could be purer or more exalted than a love of that kind?"

Having uttered this eloquent preface, which was, indeed, characteristic of the fair creature, Aurora told Aunt Eliza of the bassoon, and as she spoke of his versatile accomplishments and admirable qualities her eyes glowed with an unwonted animation, and a carmine hue suffused her beautiful cheeks. It was plain that Aurora was deeply in love, and Aunt Eliza was overjoyed.

"It is gratifying," said Aunt Eliza, "to find that my teachings promise such happy results, that the seeds I have so carefully sown already show signs of a glorious fruition. Now, while it is true that I cannot conceive of a happier love than that which exists between my own dear tabby cat and myself, it is also true that I recognize your bassoon as an object so much worthier of adoration than mankind in general, and your male acquaintances in particular, that I most heartily felicitate you upon the idol you have chosen for your worship. Bassoons do not smoke, nor chew tobacco, nor swear, nor bet on horse-races, nor play billiards, nor do any of those horrid things which constitute the larger part of a man's ambitions and pursuits. You have acted wisely, my dear, and heaven grant you may be as happy in his love as I am in tabby's."

"I feel that I shall be," murmured Aurora; "already my bassoon is very precious to me."

With the dawn of this first passion a new motive seemed to come into Aurora's life—a gentle melancholy, a subdued sentiment whose accompaniments were sighings and day-dreamings and solitary tears and swoonings.

Quite naturally Aurora sought Aunt Eliza's society more than ever now, and her conversation and thoughts were always on the bassoon. It was very beautiful.

But late one night Aurora burst into Aunt Eliza's room and threw herself upon Aunt Eliza's bed, sobbing bitterly. Aunt Eliza was inexpressibly shocked, and under a sudden impulse of horror the tabby sprang to her feet, arched her back, bristled her tail, and uttered monosyllables of astonishment.

"Why, Aurora, what ails you?" inquired Aunt Eliza, kindly.

"Oh, auntie, my heart is broken, I know it is," wailed Aurora.

"Come, come, my child," said Aunt Eliza, soothingly, "don't take on so. Tell auntie what ails you."

"He was harsh and cruel to me to-night, and oh! I loved him so!" moaned Aurora.

"A lovers' quarrel, eh?" thought Aunt Eliza; and she got up, slipped her wrapper on, and brewed Aurora a big bowl of boneset tea. Oh, how nice and bitter and fragrant it was, and how Aunt Eliza's nostrils sniffed, and how her eyes sparkled as she sipped the grateful beverage.

"There, drink that, my dear," said Aunt Eliza, "and then tell me all about it."

Aurora quaffed the bowl of boneset tea, and the wholesome draught seemed to give her fortitude, for now she told Aunt Eliza the whole story. It seems that Aurora had been to the opera as usual, not for the purpose of hearing and seeing the performance, but simply for the sake of being where the beloved bassoon was. The opera was Wagner's "Die Walküre," and the part played by the bassoon in the orchestration was one of conspicuous importance. Fully appreciating his importance, the bassoon conducted himself with brutal arrogance and superciliousness on this occasion. His whole nature seemed changed; his tones were harsh and discordant, and with malevolent obstinacy he led all the other instruments in the orchestra through a seemingly endless series of musical pyrotechnics. There never was a more remarkable exhibition of stubbornness. When the violins and the 'cellos, the hautboys and the flutes, the cornets and the trombones, said "Come, let us work together in G minor," or "Let us do this passage in B flat," the bassoon would lead off with a wild shriek in D sharp or some other foreign key, and maintain it so lustily that the other instruments—e. g., the violins, the 'cellos, the hautboys, and all—were compelled to back, switch, and wheel into the bassoon's lead as best they could.

But no sooner had they come into harmony than the bassoon—oh, melancholy perversity of that instrument—would strike off into another key with a ribald snicker or coarse guffaw, causing more turbulence and another stampede. And this preposterous condition of affairs was kept up the whole evening, the bassoon seeming to take a fiendish delight in his riotous, brutal conduct.

At first Aurora was mortified; then her mortification deepened into chagrin. In the hope of touching his heart she bestowed upon him a look of such tender supplication that, had he not been the most callous creature in the world, he must have melted under it. To his eternal shame, let it be said, the bassoon remained as impervious to her beseeching glances as if he had been a sphinx or a rhinoceros. In fact, Aurora's supplicating eyes seemed to instigate him to further and greater madness, for after that he became still more riotous, and at many times during the evening the crisis in the orchestra threatened anarchy and general disintegration.

Aurora's humiliation can be imagined by those only who have experienced a like bitterness—the bitterness of awakening to a realization of the cruelty of love. Aurora loved the bassoon tenderly, deeply, absorbingly. The sprightliness of his lighter moods, no less than the throbbing pathos of his sadder moments, had won her heart. She had given him her love unreservedly, she fairly worshipped him, and now she awakened, as it were, from a golden dream, to find her idol clay! It was very sad. Yet who that has loved either man or bassoon does not know this bitterness?

"He will be gentler hereafter," said Aunt Eliza, encouragingly. "You must always remember that we should be charitable and indulgent with those we love. Who knows why the bassoon was harsh and wayward and imperious to-night? Let us not judge him till we have heard the whys and wherefores. He may have been ill; depend upon it, my dear, he had cause for his conduct."

Aunt Eliza's prudent words were a great solace to Aurora. And she forgave the bassoon all the pain he had inflicted when she went to the opera the next night and heard him in "I Puritani," a work in which the grand virility of his nature, its vigor and force, came out with telling effect. There was not a trace of the insolence he had manifested in "Die Walküre," nor of the humorous antics he had displayed in "La Grande Duchesse"; divested of all charlatanism, he was now a magnificent, sonorous, manly bassoon, and you may depend upon it Aurora was more in love with him than ever.

It was about this time that, perceiving a marked change in his daughter's appearance and demeanor, Aurora's father began to question her mother about it all, and that good lady at last made bold to tell the old gentleman the whole truth of the matter, which was simply that Aurora cherished a passion for the bassoon. Now the father was an exceedingly matter-of-fact, old-fashioned man, who possessed not the least bit of sentiment, and when he heard that his only child had fallen in love with a bassoon, his anger was very great. He summoned Aurora into his presence, and regarded her with an austere countenance.

"Girl," he said, in icy tones, "is it true that you have been flirting with a bassoon?"

"Father," replied Aurora, with dignity, "I have never flirted with anybody, and you grievously wrong the bassoon when you intimated that he, too, is capable of such frivolity."

"It is nevertheless true," roared the old gentleman, "that you have conceived a passion for this bassoon, and have cherished it clandestinely."

"It is true, father, that I love the bassoon," said Aurora; "it is true that I admire his wit, vivacity, sentiment, soul, force, power, and manliness, but I have loved in secret. We have never met; he may know I love him, and he may reciprocate my love, but he has never spoken to me nor I to him, so there is nothing clandestine in the affair."

"Oh, my child! my child!" sobbed the old man, breaking down; "how could you love a bassoon, when so many eligible young men are suitors for your hand?"

"Don't mention him in the same breath with those horrid creatures!" cried Aurora, indignantly. "What scent of tobacco or odor of wines has ever profaned the purity of his balmy breath? What does he know of billiards, of horse-racing, of actresses, and those other features of brutal men's lives? Father, he is pure and good and exalted; seek not to debase him by naming him in the category of man!"

"These are Eliza's teachings!" shrieked the old gentleman; and off he bundled to vent his wrath on the maiden aunt. But it was little satisfaction he got from Aunt Eliza.

After that the old gentleman kept a strict eye on Aurora, and very soon he became satisfied of two things: First, that Aurora was sincerely in love with the bassoon; and, second, that the bassoon cared nothing for Aurora. That Aurora loved the bassoon was evidenced by her demeanor when in his presence—her steadfast eyes, her parted lips, her heaving bosom, her piteous sighs, her flushed cheeks, and her varying emotions as his tones changed, bore unimpeachable testimony to the sincerity of her passion. That the bassoon did not care for Aurora was proved by his utter disregard of her feelings, for though he might be tender this moment he was harsh the next—though pleading now he spurned her anon; and so, variable and fickle and false as the winds, he kept Aurora in misery and hysterics about half the time.

One morning the old gentleman entered the theatre while the orchestra was rehearsing.

"Who plays the bassoon?" he asked, in an imperative tone.

"Ich!" said a man with a bald head and gold spectacles.

"Your name?" demanded the old gentleman.

"Otto Baumgarten," replied he of the bald head and gold spectacles.

"Then, Otto Baumgarten," said the father, "I will give you one hundred dollars for your bassoon."

"Mein Gott!" said Herr Baumgarten, "dat bassoon gost me not half so much fon dot!"

"Never mind!" replied the old gentleman. "Take the money and give me the bassoon."

Herr Baumgarten did not hesitate a moment. He clutched at the gold pieces, and while he counted them Aurora's father was hastening up the street with the bassoon under his arm. Aurora saw him coming, and she recognized the idol of her soul; his silver-plated keys were not to be mistaken. With a cry of joy she met her father in the hallway, snatched the bassoon to her heart, and covered him with kisses.

"He makes no answer to your protestations!" said her father. "Come, give over a love that is hopeless; cast aside this bassoon, who is hollow at heart, and whose affection at best is only platonic!"

"You speak blasphemies, father," cried Aurora, "and you yourself shall hear how he loves me, for when I but put my lips to this slender mouthpiece there shall issue from my worshipped bassoon tones of such ineffable tenderness that even you shall be convinced that my passion is reciprocated."

With these words Aurora glued her beauteous lips to the slender blowpipe of the bassoon, and, having inflated her lungs to their capacity, breathed into it a respiration that seemed to come from her very soul. But no sound issued from the cold, hollow, unresponsive bassoon. Aurora repeated the effort with increased vigor. There came no answer at all.

"Aha!" laughed her father. "I told you so; he loves you not."

But then, with a last superhuman effort, Aurora made her third attempt; her eyeballs started from their sockets, big, blue veins and cords stood out on her lovely neck, and all the force and vigor of her young life seemed to go out through her pursed lips into the bassoon's system. And then, oh then! as if to mock her idolatry and sound the death knell of her unhappy love, the bassoon recoiled and emitted a tone so harsh, so discordant, so supernatural, that even Aurora's father drew back in horror.

And lo! hearing that supernatural sound that told her of the hopelessness of love, Aurora dropped the hollow, mocking scoffer, clutched spasmodically at her heart, and, with an agonizing shriek, fell lifeless to the floor.

I

THE EEL-KING

There was a maiden named Liliokani whose father was a fisherman. But the maiden liked not her father's employment, for she believed it to be an offence against Atua, the all-god, to deprive any animal of that life which Atua had breathed into it. And this was pleasing unto Atua, and he blessed Liliokani with exceeding beauty; no other eyes were so large, dark, and tender as hers; the braids of her long, soft hair fell like silken seagrass upon her shoulders; she was tall and graceful as the palm, and her voice was the voice of the sea when the sea cradles the moonlight and sings it to sleep.

Full many kings' sons came wooing Liliokani, and chiefs renowned in war; and with others came Tatatao, that was a mighty hunter of hares and had compassed famous hardships. For those men that delight in adventure and battle are most pleasantly minded to gentle women, for thus capriciously hath Atua, the all-god, ordained. But Liliokani had no ear to the wooing of these men, and the fisherman's daughter was a virgin when Mimi came.

Mimi was king of the eels, and Atua had given him eternal life and the power to change his shape when it pleased him to issue from the water and walk the earth. It befell that this eel-king, Mimi, beheld Liliokani upon a time as he swam the little river near her father's abode, and he saw that she was exceeding fair and he heard the soft, sad sea-tone in her voice. So for many days Mimi frequented those parts and grew more and more in love with the maiden.

Upon a certain day, while she helped her father to mend his nets, Liliokani saw a young man of goodly stature and handsome face approaching, and to herself she said: "Surely if ever I be tempted to wed it shall be with this young man, whose like I have never before known." But she had no thought that it was Mimi, the eel-king, who in this changed shape now walked the earth.

Sweetly he made obeisance and pleasant was his discourse with the fisherman and his daughter, and he told them many things of his home, which he said was many kumes distant from that spot. Though he spake mostly to the old man, his eyes were fixed upon Liliokani, and, after the fashion of her sex, that maiden presently knew that he had great love unto her. Many days after that came Mimi to hold discourse with them, and they had joy of his coming, for in sooth he was of fair countenance and sweet address, and the fisherman, being a single-minded and a simple man, had no suspicion of the love between Mimi and Liliokani. But once Mimi said to Liliokani in such a voice as the sea-wind hath to the maiden palm-trees: "Brown maiden mine, let thy door be unlatched this night, and I will come to thee."

So the door was not latched that night and Mimi went in unto her, and they two were together and alone.

"What meaneth that moaning of the sea?" asked Liliokani.

"The sea chanteth our bridal anthem," he answered.

"And what sad music cometh from the palms to-night?" she asked.

"They sing soft and low of our wedded love," he answered.

But Liliokani apprehended evil, and, although she spake no more of it at that time, a fear of trouble was in her heart.

Now Atua, the all-god, was exceeding wroth at this thing, and in grievous anger he beheld how that every night the door was unlatched and Mimi went in unto Liliokani. And Atua set about to do vengeance, and Atua's wrath is sure and very dreadful.

There was a night when Mimi did not come; the door was unlatched and the breath of Liliokani was as the perfume of flowers and of spices commingled; yet he came not. Then Liliokani wept and unbraided her hair and cried as a widow crieth, and she thought that Mimi had found another pleasanter than she unto him. So, upon the next night, she latched the door. But in the middle of the night, when the fire was kindled in the island moon, there was a gentle tapping at the door, and Mimi called to her. And when she had unlatched the door she began to chide him, but he stopped her chiding, and with great groaning he took her to his breast, and she knew by the beating of his heart that evil had come upon him.

Then Mimi told her who he was and how wroth the all-god was because the eel-king, forgetful of his immortality and neglectful of his domain, loved the daughter of a mortal.

"Forswear me, then," quoth Liliokani, "forswear me, and come not hither again, and the anger of the all-god shall be appeased."

"It is not to lie to Atua," answered Mimi. "The all-god readeth every heart and knoweth every thought. How can I, that love thee only, forswear thee? More just and terrible would be Atua's wrath for that lie to him and that wrong to thee and to myself. Brown maiden, I go back into the sea and from thee forever, bearing with me a love for thee which even the all-god's anger cannot chill."

So he kissed her for the last time and bade her a last farewell, and then he went from that door down to the water's edge and into his domain. And Liliokani made great moan and her heart was like to break. But the sea was placid as a hearthstone and the palms lay asleep in the sky that night, for it was Atua's will that the woman should suffer alone.

In the middle of the next night a mighty tempest arose. The clouds reached down and buffeted the earth and sea, and the winds and the waters cried out in anger against each other and smote each other. Above the tumult Atua's voice was heard. "Arise, Liliokani," quoth that voice, "and with thy father's stone hatchet smite off the head of the fish that lieth upon the threshold of the door."

Then Liliokani arose with fear and trembling and went to the door, and there, on the threshold, lay a monster eel whose body had been floated thither by the flood and the tempest. With her father's stone hatchet she smote off the eel's head, and the head fell into the hut, but the long, dead body floated back with the flood into the sea and was seen no more. Then the tempest abated, and with the morning came the sun's light and its tender warmth. And at the earliest moment Liliokani took the eel's head secretly and buried it with much sorrow and weeping, for the eyes within that lifeless head were Mimi's eyes, and Liliokani knew that this thing was come of the all-god's wrath.

It was her wont to go each day and make moan over the spot where she had hid this vestige of her love, and presently Atua pitied her, for Atua loveth his children upon this earth, even though they sin most grievously. So, by and by, Liliokani saw that two green leaves were sprouting from the earth, and in a season these two leaves became twin stalks and grew into trees, the like of which had never before been seen upon earth. And Liliokani lived to see and to taste the fruit of these twin trees that sprung from Mimi's brain—the red cocoanut and the white cocoanut, whereof all men have eaten since that time. And all folk hold that fruit in sweet estimation, for it cometh from the love that a god had unto a mortal woman, and mortality is love and love is immortality.

Atua forgot not Liliokani when the skies opened to her; she liveth forever in the star that looketh only upon this island, and it is her tender grace that nourishes the infant cocoas and maketh the elder ones fruitful. Meanwhile no woman that dwelleth upon earth hath satisfaction in tasting the flesh of eels, for a knowledge of Mimi's love and sacrifice hath been subtly implanted by Atua, the all-god, in every woman's breast.

II

THE MOON LADY

Once there were four maidens who were the daughters of Talakoa, and they were so very beautiful that their fame spread through the universe. The oldest of these maidens was named Kaulualua, and it is of her that it is to tell this tale.

One day while Kaulualua was combing her hair she saw a tall, fair man fishing in the rivulet, and he was a stranger to her. Never before had she seen so fair a man, though in very sooth she had been wooed of many king's sons and of chiefs from every part of the earth. Then she called to her three sisters and asked them his name, but they could not answer; this, however, they knew—he was of no country whereof they had heard tell, for he was strangely clad and he was of exceeding fair complexion and his stature surpassed that of other men.

The next day these maidens saw this same tall, fair man, but he no longer fished in the rivulet; he hunted the hares and was passing skilful thereat, so that the maidens admired him not only for his exceeding comeliness but also for his skill as a huntsman, for surely there was no hare that could escape his vigilance and the point of his arrow. So when Talakoa, their father, came that evening the maidens told him of this stranger, and he wondered who he was and whence he fared. Awaking from sleep in the middle of that night, Kaulualua saw that the stars shone with rare brilliancy, and that by their light a man was gazing upon her through the window. And she saw that the man was the tall, fair man of whom it has been spoken. So she uttered no cry, but feigned that she slept, for she saw that there was love in the tall, fair man's eyes, and it pleaseth a maiden to be looked upon in that wise.

When it was morning this tall, fair man came and entered that house and laid a fish and a hare upon the hearthstone and called for Talakoa. And he quoth to Talakoa:

"Old man, I would have your daughter to wife."

Being a full crafty man, as beseemeth one of years, Talakoa replied: "Four daughters have I."

The tall, fair man announced: "You speak sooth, as well becometh a full crafty man. Four daughters have you, and it is Kaulualua that I would have to wife."

Saith that full crafty man, the father: "How many palm trees grow in thy possession, and how many rivers flow through thy chiefdom? Whence comest thou, gentle sir, for assuredly neither I nor mine have seen the like of thee before."

"Good sooth," answered the tall, fair man, "I will tell you no lie, for I would have that daughter to wife, and the things you require do well beseem a full crafty man that meaneth for his child's good. I am the man of the moon, and my name is Marama."

Then Talakoa and his daughters looked at one another and were sore puzzled, for they knew not whereof Marama spake. And they deemed him a madman; yet did they not laugh him to scorn, because that he had come a-wooing, and had laid the fish and the hare upon the hearthstone.

"Kind sir, bringing gifts," quoth Talakoa, "I say no lie to you, but we know not that country whereof you speak. Pray tell us of the moon and where is it situate, and how many kumes is it distant from here?"

"Full crafty man, father of her whom I would have to wife, I will tell you truly," answered Marama. "The moon wherefrom I come is a mighty island in the vast sea of night, and it is distant from here so great a space that it were not to count the kumes that lie between. Exceeding fair is that island in that vast sea, and it hath mountains and valleys and plains and seas and rivers and lakes, and I am the chief overall. Atua made that island for me and put it in that mighty sea, for I am the son of Atua, and over that island in that sea I shall rule forever."

Great wonder had they to hear tell of these things, and they knew now that Marama was the child of Atua, who made the universe and is the all-god. Then Marama said on:

"Atua bade me search and find me a wife, and upon the stars have I walked two hundred years, fishing and hunting, and seeing maidens, but of all maidens seen there is none that I did love. So now at last, in this island of this earth, I have found Kaulualua, and have seen the pearl of her beauty and smelled the cinnamon of her breath, and I would fain have her to wife that she may be ruler with me over the moon, my island in the vast, black sea of night."

It was not for Talakoa, being of earth such as all human kind, to gainsay the words of Marama. And there was a flame in Kaulualua's heart and incense in her breath and honey in her eyes toward this tall, fair man that was the son of Atua. So the old father said to her: "Take up the fish and the hare and roast them, my daughter, and spread them before us, and we will eat them and so pledge our troth, one to another."

This thing did Kaulualua, and so the man from the moon had her to wife.

That night they went from the home of Talakoa to the island in the sea of night, and Talakoa and the three maidens watched for a signal from that island, for Kaulualua told them she would build a fire thereon that they might know when she was come thither. Many, many nights they watched, and their hair grew white, and Time marked their faces with his fingers, and the moss gathered on the palm trees. At last, as if he would sleep forever, Talakoa laid himself upon his mat by the door and asked that the skies be opened to him, for he was enfeebled with age.

And while he asked this thing the three sisters saw a dim light afar off in the black sea of night, and it was such a light as had never before been seen. And this light grew larger and brighter, so that in seven nights it was thrice the size of the largest palm leaf, and it lighted up all that far-off island in the sea of night, and they knew that Kaulualua and the moon-god were in their home at last. So old Talakoa was soothed and the skies that opened unto him found him satisfied.

The three sisters lived long, and yet two hundred ages are gone since the earth received them into its bosom. Yet still upon that island in the dark sea of night abideth in love the moon-god with his bride. Atua hath been good to her, for he hath given her eternal youth, as he giveth to all wives that do truly love and serve their husbands. It is for us to see that pleasant island wherein Kaulualua liveth; it is for us to see that when Marama goeth abroad to hunt or to fish his moon-lady sitteth alone and maketh moan, and heedeth not her fires; it is for us to see that when anon he cometh back she buildeth up those fires whereon to cook food for him, and presently the fires grow brighter and the whole round moon island is lighted and warmed thereby. In this wise an exceeding fair example is set unto all wives of their duty unto their mates.

When the sea singeth to the sands, when the cane beckoneth to the stars, and when the palm-leaves whisper to sweet-breathed night, how pleasant it is, my brown maiden, to stand with thee and look upon that island in the azure sea that spreadeth like a veil above the cocoa trees. For there we see the moon-lady, and she awaiteth her dear lord and she smileth in love; and that grace warmeth our hearts—your heart and mine, O little maiden! and we are glad with a joy that knoweth no speaking.

LUTE BAKER AND HIS WIFE EM

The Plainfield boys always had the name of being smart, and I guess Lute Baker was just about the smartest boy the old town ever turned out. Well, he came by it naturally; Judge Baker was known all over western Massachusetts as the sage of Plainfield, and Lute's mother—she was a Kellogg before the judge married her—she had more faculty than a dozen of your girls nowadays, and her cooking was talked about everywhere—never was another woman, as folks said, could cook like Miss Baker. The boys—Lute's friends—used to hang around the back porch of noonings just to get some of her doughnuts; she was always considerate and liberal to growing boys. May be Lute would n't have been so popular if it had n't been for those doughnuts, and may be he would n't have been so smart if it had n't been for all the good things his mother fed into him. Always did believe there was piety and wisdom in New England victuals.

Lute went to Amherst College and did well; was valedictorian; then he taught school a winter, for Judge Baker said that nobody could amount to much in the world unless he taught school a spell. Lute was set on being a lawyer, and so presently he went down to Springfield and read and studied in Judge Morris' office, and Judge Morris wrote a letter home to the Bakers once testifying to Lute's "probity" and "acumen"—things that are never heard tell of except high up in the legal profession.

How Lute came to get the western fever I can't say, but get it he did, and one winter he up and piked off to Chicago, and there he hung out his shingle and joined a literary social and proceeded to get rich and famous. The next spring Judge Baker fell off the woodshed while he was shingling it, and it jarred him so he kind of drooped and pined round a spell and then one day up and died. Lute had to come back home and settle up the estate.

When he went west again he took a wife with him—Emma Cowles that was (everybody called her Em for short), pretty as a picture and as likely a girl as there was in the township. Lute had always had a hankering for Em, and Em thought there never was another such a young fellow as Lute; she understood him perfectly, having sung in the choir with him two years. The young couple went west well provided.

Lute and Em went to housekeeping in Chicago. Em wanted to do her own work, but Lute would n't hear to it; so they hired a German girl that was just over from the vineyards of the Rhine country.

"Lute," says Em, "Hulda does n't know much about cooking."

"So I see," says Lute, feelingly. "She's green as grass; you'll have to teach her."

Hulda could swing a hoe and wield a spade deftly, but of the cuisine she knew somewhat less than nothing. Em had lots of patience and pluck, but she found teaching Hulda how to cook a precious hard job. Lute was amiable enough at first; used to laugh it off with a cordial bet that by and by Em would make a famous cook of the obtuse but willing immigrant. This moral backing buoyed Em up considerable, until one evening in an unguarded moment Lute expressed a pining for some doughnuts "like those mother makes," and that casual remark made Em unhappy. But next evening when Lute came home there were doughnuts on the table—beautiful, big, plethoric doughnuts that fairly reeked with the homely, delicious sentiment of New England. Lute ate one. Em felt hurt.

"I guess it's because I 've eaten so much else," explained Lute, "but somehow or other they don't taste like mother's."

Next day Em fed the rest of the doughnuts to a poor man who came and said he was starving. "Thank you, marm," said he, with his heart full of gratitude and his mouth full of doughnuts; "I ha' n't had anything as good as this since I left Connecticut twenty years ago."

That little subtlety consoled Em, but still she found it hard to bear up under her apparent inability to do her duty by Lute's critical palate. Once when Lute brought Col. Hi Thomas home to dinner they had chicken pie. The colonel praised it and passed his plate a third time.

"Oh, but you ought to eat some of mother's chicken pie," said Lute. "Mother never puts an under crust in her chicken pies, and that makes 'em juicier."

Same way when they had fried pork and potatoes; Lute could not understand why the flesh of the wallowing, carnivorous western hog should n't be as white and firm and sweet as the meat of the swill-fed Yankee pig. And why were the Hubbard squashes so tasteless and why was maple syrup so very different? Yes, amid all his professional duties Lute found time to note and remark upon this and other similar things, and of course Em was—by implication, at least—held responsible for them all.

And Em did try so hard, so very hard, to correct the evils and to answer the hypercritical demands of Lute's foolishly petted and spoiled appetite. She warred valorously with butchers, grocers, and hucksters; she sent down east to Mother Baker for all the famous family recipes; she wrestled in speech and in practice with that awful Hulda; she experimented long and patiently; she blistered her pretty face and burned her little hands over that kitchen range—yes, a slow, constant martyrdom that conscientious wife willingly endured for years in her enthusiastic determination to do her duty by Lute. Doughnuts, chicken-pies, boiled dinners, layer-cakes, soda biscuits, flapjacks, fish balls, baked beans, squash pies, corned-beef hash, dried-apple sauce, currant wine, succotash, brown bread—how valorously Em toiled over them, only to be rewarded with some cruel reminder of how "mother" used to do these things! It was terrible; a tedious martyrdom.

Lute—mind you—Lute was not wilfully cruel; no, he was simply and irremediably a heedless idiot of a man, just as every married man is, for a spell, at least. But it broke Em's heart, all the same.

Lute's mother came to visit them when their first child was born, and she lifted a great deal of trouble off the patient wife. Old Miss Baker always liked Em; had told the minister three years ago that she knew Em would make Lute a good Christian wife. They named the boy Moses, after the old judge who was dead, and old Miss Baker said he should have his gran'pa's watch when he got to be twenty-one.

Old Miss Baker always stuck by Em; may be she remembered how the old judge had talked once on a time about his mother's cooking. For all married men are, as I have said, idiotically cruel about that sort of thing. Yes, old Miss Baker braced Em up wonderful; brought a lot of dried catnip out west with her for the baby; taught Em how to make salt-rising bread; told her all about stewing things and broiling things and roasting things; showed her how to tell the real Yankee codfish from the counterfeit—oh, she just did Em lots of good, did old Miss Baker!

The rewards of virtue may be slow in coming, but they are sure to come. Em's three boys—the three bouncing boys that came to Em and Lute—those three boys waxed fat and grew up boisterous, blatant appreciators of their mother's cooking. The way those boys did eat mother's doughnuts! And mother's pies—wow! Other boys—the neighbors' boys—came round regularly in troops, battalions, armies, and like a consuming fire licked up the wholesome viands which Em's skill and liberality provided for her own boys' enthusiastic playmates. And all those boys—there must have been millions of 'em—were living, breathing, vociferous testimonials to the unapproachable excellence of Em's cooking.

Lute got into politics, and they elected him to the legislature. After the campaign, needing rest, he took it into his head to run down east to see his mother; he had not been back home for eight years. He took little Moses with him. They were gone about three weeks. Gran'ma Baker had made great preparations for them; had cooked up enough pies to last all winter, and four plump, beheaded, well-plucked, yellow-legged pullets hung stiff and solemn-like in the chill pantry off the kitchen, awaiting the last succulent scene of all.

Lute and the little boy got there late of an evening. The dear old lady was so glad to see them; the love that beamed from her kindly eyes well nigh melted the glass in her silver-bowed specks. The table was spread in the dining-room; the sheet-iron stove sighed till it seemed like to crack with the heat of that hardwood fire.

"Why, Lute, you ain't eatin' enough to keep a fly alive," remonstrated old Miss Baker, when her son declined a second doughnut; "and what ails the child?" she continued; "ha' n't he got no appetite? Why, when you wuz his age, Lute, seemed as if I could n't cook doughnuts fast enough for you!"

Lute explained that both he and his little boy had eaten pretty heartily on the train that day. But all the time of their visit there poor old Gran'ma Baker wondered and worried because they did n't eat enough—seemed to her as if western folks had n't the right kind of appetite. Even the plump pullets, served in a style that had made Miss Baker famed throughout those discriminating parts—even those pullets failed to awaken the expected and proper enthusiasm in the visitors.

Home again in Chicago, Lute drew his chair up to the table with an eloquent sigh of relief. As for little Moses, he clamored his delight.

"Chicken pie!" he cried, gleefully; and then he added a soulful "wow!" as his eager eyes fell upon a plateful of hot, exuberant, voluptuous doughnuts.

"Yes, we are both glad to get back," said Lute.

"But I am afraid," suggested Em, timidly, "that gran'ma's cooking has spoiled you."

Little Moses (bless him) howled an indignant, a wrathful remonstrance. "Gran'ma can't cook worth a cent!" said he.

Em expected Lute to be dreadfully shocked, but he was n't.

"I would n't let her know it for all the world," remarked Lute, confidentially, "but mother has lost her grip on cooking. At any rate, her cooking is n't what it used to be; it has changed."

Then Em came bravely to the rescue. "No, Lute," says she, and she meant it, "your mother's cooking has n't changed, but you have. The man has grown away from the boy, and the tastes, the ways, and the delights of boyhood have no longer any fascination for the man."

"May be you 're right," said Lute. "At any rate, I 'm free to say that your cooking beats the world."

Good for Lute! Virtue triumphs and my true story ends. But first an explanation to concinnate my narrative.

I should never have known this true story if Lute himself had n't told it to me at the last dinner of the Sons of New England—told it to me right before Em, that dear, patient little martyred wife of his. And I knew by the love light in Em's eyes that she was glad that she had endured that martyrdom for Lute's sake.

JOEL'S TALK WITH SANTA CLAUS

One Christmas eve Joel Baker was in a most unhappy mood. He was lonesome and miserable; the chimes making merry Christmas music outside disturbed rather than soothed him, the jingle of the sleigh-bells fretted him, and the shrill whistling of the wind around the corners of the house and up and down the chimney seemed to grate harshly on his ears.

"Humph," said Joel, wearily, "Christmas is nothin' to me; there was a time when it meant a great deal, but that was long ago—fifty years is a long stretch to look back over. There is nothin' in Christmas now, nothin' for me at least; it is so long since Santa Claus remembered me that I venture to say he has forgotten that there ever was such a person as Joel Baker in all the world. It used to be different; Santa Claus used to think a great deal of me when I was a boy. Ah! Christmas nowadays ain't what it was in the good old time—no, not what it used to be."

As Joel was absorbed in his distressing thoughts he became aware very suddenly that somebody was entering or trying to enter the room. First came a draft of cold air, then a scraping, grating sound, then a strange shuffling, and then—yes, then, all at once, Joel saw a pair of fat legs and a still fatter body dangle down the chimney, followed presently by a long white beard, above which appeared a jolly red nose and two bright twinkling eyes, while over the head and forehead was drawn a fur cap, white with snowflakes.

"Ha, ha," chuckled the fat, jolly stranger, emerging from the chimney and standing well to one side of the hearthstone; "ha, ha, they don't have the big, wide chimneys they used to build, but they can't keep Santa Claus out—no, they can't keep Santa Claus out! Ha, ha, ha. Though the chimney were no bigger than a gas pipe, Santa Claus would slide down it!"

It didn't require a second glance to assure Joel that the new-comer was indeed Santa Claus. Joel knew the good old saint—oh, yes—and he had seen him once before, and, although that was when Joel was a little boy, he had never forgotten how Santa Claus looked.

Nor had Santa Claus forgotten Joel, although Joel thought he had; for now Santa Claus looked kindly at Joel and smiled and said: "Merry Christmas to you, Joel!"

"Thank you, old Santa Claus," replied Joel, "but I don't believe it's going to be a very merry Christmas. It's been so long since I 've had a merry Christmas that I don't believe I 'd know how to act if I had one."

"Let's see," said Santa Claus, "it must be going on fifty years since I saw you last—yes, you were eight years old the last time I slipped down the chimney of the old homestead and filled your stocking. Do you remember it?"

"I remember it well," answered Joel. "I had made up my mind to lie awake and see Santa Claus; I had heard tell of you, but I 'd never seen you, and Brother Otis and I concluded we 'd lie awake and watch for you to come."

Santa Claus shook his head reproachfully. "That was very wrong," said he, "for I 'm so scarey that if I 'd known you boys were awake I 'd never have come down the chimney at all, and then you 'd have had no presents."

"But Otis could n't keep awake," explained Joel. "We talked about everythin' we could think of, till father called out to us that if we did n't stop talking he 'd have to send one of us up into the attic to sleep with the hired man. So in less than five minutes Otis was sound asleep and no pinching could wake him up. But I was bound to see Santa Claus and I don't believe anything would 've put me to sleep. I heard the big clock in the sitting-room strike eleven, and I had begun wonderin' if you never were going to come, when all of a sudden I heard the tinkle of the bells around your reindeers' necks. Then I heard the reindeers prancin' on the roof and the sound of your sleigh-runners cuttin' through the crust and slippin' over the shingles. I was kind o' scared and I covered my head up with the sheet and quilts—only I left a little hole so I could peek out and see what was goin' on. As soon as I saw you I got over bein' scared—for you were jolly and smilin' like, and you chuckled as you went around to each stockin' and filled it up."

"Yes, I can remember the night," said Santa Claus. "I brought you a sled, did n't I?"

"Yes, and you brought Otis one, too," replied Joel. "Mine was red and had 'Yankee Doodle' painted in black letters on the side; Otis' was black and had 'Snow Queen' in gilt letters."

"I remember those sleds distinctly," said Santa Claus, "for I made them specially for you boys."

"You set the sleds up against the wall," continued Joel, "and then you filled the stockin's."

"There were six of 'em, as I recollect?" said Santa Claus.

"Let me see," queried Joel. "There was mine, and Otis', and Elvira's, and Thankful's, and Susan Prickett's—Susan was our help, you know. No, there were only five, and, as I remember, they were the biggest we could beg or borrer of Aunt Dorcas, who weighed nigh unto two hundred pounds. Otis and I did n't like Susan Prickett, and we were hopin' you 'd put a cold potato in her stockin'."

"But Susan was a good girl," remonstrated Santa Claus. "You know I put cold potatoes only in the stockin's of boys and girls who are bad and don't believe in Santa Claus."

"At any rate," said Joel, "you filled all the stockin's with candy and pop-corn and nuts and raisins, and I can remember you said you were afraid you 'd run out of pop-corn balls before you got around. Then you left each of us a book. Elvira got the best one, which was 'The Garland of Frien'ship,' and had poems in it about the bleeding of hearts, and so forth. Father was n't expectin' anything, but you left him a new pair of mittens, and mother got a new fur boa to wear to meetin'."

"Of course," said Santa Claus, "I never forgot father and mother."

"Well, it was as much as I could do to lay still," continued Joel, "for I 'd been longin' for a sled, an' the sight of that red sled with 'Yankee Doodle' painted on it jest made me wild. But, somehow or other, I began to get powerful sleepy all at once, and I could n't keep my eyes open. The next thing I knew Otis was nudgin' me in the ribs. 'Git up, Joel,' says he; 'it's Chris'mas an' Santa Claus has been here.' 'Merry Christ'mas! Merry Chris'mas!' we cried as we tumbled out o' bed. Then Elvira an' Thankful came in, not more 'n half dressed, and Susan came in, too, an' we just made Rome howl with 'Merry Chris'mas! Merry Chris'mas!' to each other. 'Ef you children don't make less noise in there,' cried father, 'I'll hev to send you all back to bed.' The idea of askin' boys an' girls to keep quiet on Chris'mas mornin' when they 've got new sleds an' 'Garlands of Frien'ship'!"

Santa Claus chuckled; his rosy cheeks fairly beamed joy.

"Otis an' I did n't want any breakfast," said Joel. "We made up our minds that a stockin'ful of candy and pop-corn and raisins would stay us for a while. I do believe there was n't buckwheat cakes enough in the township to keep us indoors that mornin'; buckwheat cakes don't size up much 'longside of a red sled with 'Yankee Doodle' painted onto it and a black sled named 'Snow Queen.' We did n't care how cold it was—so much the better for slidin' down hill! All the boys had new sleds—Lafe Dawson, Bill Holbrook, Gum Adams, Rube Playford, Leander Merrick, Ezra Purple—all on 'em had new sleds excep' Martin Peavey, and he said he calculated Santa Claus had skipped him this year 'cause his father had broke his leg haulin' logs from the Pelham woods and had been kep' indoors six weeks. But Martin had his ol' sled, and he didn't hev to ask any odds of any of us, neither."

"I brought Martin a sled the next Christmas," said Santa Claus.

"Like as not—but did you ever slide down hill, Santa Claus? I don't mean such hills as they hev out here in this new country, but one of them old-fashioned New England hills that was made 'specially for boys to slide down, full of bumpers an' thank-ye-marms, and about ten times longer comin' up than it is goin' down! The wind blew in our faces and almos' took our breath away. 'Merry Chris'mas to ye, little boys!' it seemed to say, and it untied our mufflers an' whirled the snow in our faces, just as if it was a boy, too, an' wanted to play with us. An ol' crow came flappin' over us from the corn field beyond the meadow. He said: 'Caw, caw,' when he saw my new sled—I s'pose he 'd never seen a red one before. Otis had a hard time with his sled—the black one—an' he wondered why it would n't go as fast as mine would. 'Hev you scraped the paint off'n the runners?' asked Wralsey Goodnow.

'Course I hev,' said Otis; 'broke my own knife an' Lute Ingraham's a-doin' it, but it don't seem to make no dif'rence—the darned ol' thing won't go!' Then, what did Simon Buzzell say but that, like 's not, it was because Otis's sled's name was 'Snow Queen.' 'Never did see a girl sled that was worth a cent, anyway,' sez Simon. Well, now, that jest about broke Otis up in business. 'It ain't a girl sled,' sez he, 'and its name ain't "Snow Queen"! I'm a-goin' to call it "Dan'l Webster," or "Ol'ver Optic," or "Sheriff Robbins," or after some other big man!' An' the boys plagued him so much about that pesky girl sled that he scratched off the name, an', as I remember, it did go better after that!

"About the only thing," continued Joel, "that marred the harmony of the occasion, as the editor of the 'Hampshire County Phoenix' used to say, was the ashes that Deacon Morris Frisbie sprinkled out in front of his house. He said he was n't going to have folks breakin' their necks jest on account of a lot of frivolous boys that was goin' to the gallows as fas' as they could! Oh, how we hated him! and we 'd have snowballed him, too, if we had n't been afraid of the constable that lived next door. But the ashes did n't bother us much, and every time we slid sidesaddle we 'd give the ashes a kick, and that sort of scattered 'em."

The bare thought of this made Santa Claus laugh.

"Goin' on about nine o'clock," said Joel, "the girls come along—Sister Elvira an' Thankful, Prudence Tucker, Belle Yocum, Sophrone Holbrook, Sis Hubbard, an' Marthy Sawyer. Marthy's brother Increase wanted her to ride on his sled, but Marthy allowed that a red sled was her choice every time. 'I don't see how I 'm goin' to hold on,' said Marthy. 'Seems as if I would hev my hands full keepin' my things from blowin' away.' 'Don't worry about yourself, Marthy,' sez I, 'for if you'll look after your things, I kind o' calc'late I'll manage not to lose you on the way.' Dear Marthy—seems as if I could see you now, with your tangled hair a-blowin' in the wind, your eyes all bright and sparklin', an' your cheeks as red as apples. Seems, too, as if I could hear you laughin' an' callin', jist as you did as I toiled up the old New England hill that Chris'mas mornin'—a callin': 'Joel, Joel, Joel—ain't ye ever comin', Joel?' But the hill is long and steep, Marthy, an' Joel ain't the boy he used to be; he 's old, an' gray, an' feeble, but there's love an' faith in his heart, an' they kind o' keep him totterin' tow'rds the voice he hears a-callin': 'Joel, Joel, Joel!'"

"I know—I see it all," murmured Santa Claus, very softly.

"Oh, that was so long ago," sighed Joel; "so very long ago! And I've had no Chris'mas since—only once, when our little one—Marthy's an' mine—you remember him, Santa Claus?"

"Yes," said Santa Claus, "a toddling little boy with blue eyes—"

"Like his mother," interrupted Joel; "an' he was like her, too—so gentle an' lovin', only we called him Joel, for that was my father's name and it kind o' run in the fam'ly. He wa' n't more 'n three years old when you came with your Chris'mas presents for him, Santa Claus. We had told him about you, and he used to go to the chimney every night and make a little prayer about what he wanted you to bring him. And you brought 'em, too—a stick-horse, an' a picture-book, an' some blocks, an' a drum—they 're on the shelf in the closet there, and his little Chris'mas stockin' with 'em—I 've saved 'em all, an' I 've taken 'em down an' held 'em in my hands, oh, so many times!"

"But when I came again," said Santa Claus—

"His little bed was empty, an' I was alone. It killed his mother—Marthy was so tender-hearted; she kind o' drooped an' pined after that. So now they 've been asleep side by side in the buryin'-ground these thirty years.

"That's why I 'm so sad-like whenever Chris'mas comes," said Joel, after a pause. "The thinkin' of long ago makes me bitter almost. It's so different now from what it used to be."

"No, Joel, oh, no," said Santa Claus. "'T is the same world, and human nature is the same and always will be. But Christmas is for the little folks, and you, who are old and grizzled now, must know it and love it only through the gladness it brings the little ones."

"True," groaned Joel; "but how may I know and feel this gladness when I have no little stocking hanging in my chimney corner—no child to please me with his prattle? See, I am alone."

"No, you 're not alone, Joel," said Santa Claus. "There are children in this great city who would love and bless you for your goodness if you but touched their hearts. Make them happy, Joel; send by me this night some gift to the little boy in the old house yonder—he is poor and sick; a simple toy will fill his Christmas with gladness."

"His little sister, too—take her some present," said Joel; "make them happy for me, Santa Claus— you are right—make them happy for me."

How sweetly Joel slept! When he awoke, the sunlight streamed in through the window and seemed to bid him a merry Christmas. How contented and happy Joel felt! It must have been the talk with Santa Claus that did it all; he had never known a sweeter sense of peace. A little girl came out of the house over the way. She had a new doll in her arms, and she sang a merry little song and she laughed with joy as she skipped along the street. Ay, and at the window sat the little sick boy, and the toy Santa Claus left him seemed to have brought him strength and health, for his eyes sparkled and his cheeks glowed, and it was plain to see his heart was full of happiness.

And, oh! how the chimes did ring out, and how joyfully they sang their Christmas carol that morning! They sang of Bethlehem and the manger and the Babe; they sang of love and charity, till all the Christmas air seemed full of angel voices.

Carol of the Christmas morn— Carol of the Christ-child born— Carol to the list'ning sky Till it echoes back again "Glory be to God on high, Peace on earth, good will tow'rd men!"

So all this music—the carol of the chimes, the sound of children's voices, the smile of the poor little boy over the way—all this sweet music crept into Joel's heart that Christmas morning; yes, and with these sweet, holy influences came others so subtile and divine that, in its silent communion with them, Joel's heart cried out amen and amen to the glory of the Christmas time.

THE LONESOME LITTLE SHOE

The clock was in ill humor; so was the vase. It was all on account of the little shoe that had been placed on the mantel-piece that day, and had done nothing but sigh dolorously all the afternoon and evening.

"Look you here, neighbor," quoth the clock, in petulant tones, "you are sadly mistaken if you think you will be permitted to disturb our peace and harmony with your constant sighs and groans. If you are ill, pray let us know; otherwise, have done with your manifestations of distress."

"Possibly you do not know what befell the melancholy plaque that intruded his presence upon us last week," said the vase. "We pitched him off the mantelpiece, and he was shattered into a thousand bits."

The little shoe gave a dreadful shudder. It could not help thinking it had fallen among inhospitable neighbors. It began to cry. The brass candlestick took pity on the sobbing thing, and declared with some show of temper that the little shoe should not be imposed on.

"Now tell us why you are so full of sadness," said the brass candlestick.

"I do not know how to explain," whimpered the little shoe. "You see I am quite a young thing, albeit I have a rusty appearance and there is a hole in my toes and my heel is badly run over. I feel so lonesome and friendless and sort of neglected-like, that it seems as if there were nothing for me to do but sigh and grieve and weep all day long."

"Sighing and weeping do no good," remarked the vase, philosophically.

"I know that very well," replied the little shoe; "but once I was so happy that my present lonesome lot oppresses me all the more grievously."

"You say you once were happy—pray tell us all about it," demanded the brass candlestick.

The vase was eager to hear the little shoe's story, and even the proud, haughty clock expressed a willingness to listen. The matchbox came from the other end of the mantel-piece, and the pen-wiper, the paper-cutter, and the cigar-case gathered around the little shoe, and urged it to proceed with its narrative.

"The first thing I can remember in my short life," said the little shoe, "was being taken from a large box in which there were many of my kind thrown together in great confusion. I found myself tied with a slender cord to a little mate, a shoe so very like me that you could not have told us apart. We two were taken and put in a large window in the midst of many grown-up shoes, and we had nothing to do but gaze out of the window all day long into the wide, busy street. That was a very pleasant life. Sometimes the sunbeams would dance through the window-panes and play at hide-and-seek all over me and my little mate; they would kiss and caress us, and we learned to love them very much—they were so warm and gentle and merrisome. Sometimes the raindrops would patter against the window-panes, singing wild songs to us, and clamoring to break through and destroy us with their eagerness. When night came, we could see stars away up in the dark sky winking at us, and very often the old mother moon stole out from behind a cloud to give us a kindly smile. The wind used to sing us lullabies, and in one corner of our window there was a little open space where the mice gave a grand ball every night to the music of the crickets and a blind frog. Altogether we had a merry time."

"I 'd have liked it all but the wind," said the brass candlestick. "I don't know why it is, but I 'm dreadfully put out by the horrid old wind!"

"Many people," continued the little shoe, "used to stop and look in at the window, and I believe my little mate and I were admired more than any of our larger and more pretentious companions. I can remember there was a pair of red-top boots that was exceedingly jealous of us. But that did not last long, for one day a very sweet lady came and peered in at the window and smiled very joyously when she saw me and my little mate. Then I remember we were taken from the window, and the lady held us in her hands and examined us very closely, and measured our various dimensions with a string, and finally, I remember, she said she would carry us home. We did not know what that meant, only we realized that we would never live in the shop window again, and we were loath to be separated from the sunbeams and the mice and the other friends that had been so kind to us."

"What a droll little shoe!" exclaimed the vase. Whereupon the clock frowned and ticked a warning to the vase not to interrupt the little shoe in the midst of its diverting narrative.

"It is not necessary for me to tell you how we were wrapped in paper and carried a weary distance," said the little shoe; "it is sufficient to my purpose to say that, after what seemed to us an interminable journey and a cruel banging around, we were taken from the paper and found ourselves in a quiet, cozy room—yes, in this very apartment where we all are now! The sweet lady held us in her lap, and at the sweet lady's side stood a little child, gazing at us with an expression of commingled astonishment, admiration, and glee. We knew the little child belonged to the sweet lady, and from the talk we heard we knew that henceforth the child was to be our little master."

As if some sudden anguish came upon it, hushing its speech, the little shoe paused in its narrative. The others said never a word. Perhaps it was because they were beginning to understand. The proud, haughty clock seemed to be less imperious for the moment, and its ticking was softer and more reverential.

"From that time," resumed the little shoe, "our little master and we were inseparable during all the happy day. We played and danced with him and wandered everywhere through the grass, over the carpets, down the yard, up the street—ay, everywhere our little master went, we went too, sharing his pretty antics and making music everywhere. Then, when evening came and little master was put to sleep, in yonder crib, we were set on the warm carpet near his bed where we could watch him while he slept, and bid him good-morrow when the morning came. Those were pleasant nights, too, for no sooner had little master fallen asleep than the fairies came trooping through the keyholes and fluttering down the chimney to dance over his eyes all night long, giving him happy dreams, and filling his baby ears with sweetest music."

"What a curious conceit!" said the pen-wiper.

"And is it true that fairies dance on children's eyelids at night?" asked the paper-cutter.

"Certainly," the clock chimed in, "and they sing very pretty lullabies and very cunning operettas, too. I myself have seen and heard them."

"I should like to hear a fairy operetta," suggested the pen-wiper.

"I remember one the fairies sang my little master as they danced over his eyelids," said the little shoe, "and I will repeat it if you wish."

"Nothing would please me more," said the pen-wiper.

"Then you must know," said the little shoe, "that, as soon as my master fell asleep, the fairies would make their appearance, led by their queen, a most beautiful and amiable little lady no bigger than a cambric needle. Assembling on the pillow of the crib, they would order their minstrels and orchestra to seat themselves on little master's forehead. The minstrels invariably were the cricket, the flea, the katydid, and the gnat, while the orchestra consisted of mosquitos, bumblebees, and wasps. Once in a great while, on very important occasions, the fairies would bring the old blind hop-toad down the chimney and set him on the window-sill, where he would discourse droll ditties to the infinite delight of his hearers. But on ordinary occasions, the fairy queen, whose name was Taffie, would lead the performance in these pleasing words, sung to a very dulcet air:

AN INVITATION TO SLEEP

Little eyelids, cease your winking;
Little orbs, forget to beam;
Little soul, to slumber sinking,
Let the fairies rule your dream.
Breezes, through the lattice sweeping,
Sing their lullabies the while—
And a star-ray, softly creeping
To thy bedside, woos thy smile.
But no song nor ray entrancing
Can allure thee from the spell
Of the tiny fairies dancing
O'er the eyes they love so well.
See, we come in countless number—
I, their queen, and all my court—
Haste, my precious one, to slumber
Which invites our fairy sport.

"At the conclusion of this song Prince Whimwham, a tidy little gentleman fairy in pink silk small-clothes, approaching Queen Taffie and bowing graciously, would say:

Pray, lady, may I have the pleasure
Of leading you this stately measure?

To which her majesty would reply with equal graciousness in the affirmative. Then Prince Whimwham and Queen Taffie would take their places on one of my master's eyelids, and the other gentleman fairies and lady fairies would follow their example, till at last my master's face would seem to be alive with these delightful little beings. The mosquitos would blow a shrill blast on their trumpets, the orchestra would strike up, and then the festivities would begin in earnest. How the bumblebees would drone, how the wasps would buzz, and how the mosquitos would blare! It was a delightful harmony of weird sounds. The strange little dancers floated hither and thither over my master's baby face, as light as thistledowns, and as graceful as the slender plumes they wore in their hats and bonnets. Presently they would weary of dancing, and then the minstrels would be commanded to entertain them. Invariably the flea, who was a rattle-headed fellow, would discourse some such incoherent song as this:

COQUETRY

Tiddle-de-dumpty, tiddle-de-dee—
The spider courted the frisky flea;
Tiddle-de-dumpty, tiddle-de-doo—
The flea ran off with the bugaboo!
"Oh, tiddle-de-dee!"
Said the frisky flea—
For what cared she
For the miseree
The spider knew,

When, tiddle-de-doo,
The flea ran off with the bugaboo!

Rumpty-tumpty, pimplety-pan—
The flubdub courted a catamaran
But timplety-topplety, timpity-tare—
The flubdub wedded the big blue bear!
The fun began
With a pimplety-pan
When the catamaran,
Tore up a man
And streaked the air
With his gore and hair
Because the flubdub wedded the bear!

"I remember with what dignity the fairy queen used to reprove the flea for his inane levity:

Nay, futile flea; these verses you are making
Disturb the child—for, see, he is awaking!
Come, little cricket, sing your quaintest numbers,
And they, perchance, shall lull him back to slumbers.

"Upon this invitation the cricket, who is justly one of the most famous songsters in the world, would get his pretty voice in tune and sing as follows:

THE CRICKET'S SONG

When all around from out the ground
The little flowers are peeping,
And from the hills the merry rills
With vernal songs are leaping,
I sing my song the whole day long
In woodland, hedge, and thicket—
And sing it, too, the whole night through,
For I 'm a merry cricket.

The children hear my chirrup clear
As, in the woodland straying,
They gather flow'rs through summer hours—
And then I hear them saying:
"Sing, sing away the livelong day,
Glad songster of the thicket—
With your shrill mirth you gladden earth,
You merry little cricket!"

When summer goes, and Christmas snows
Are from the north returning,
I quit my lair and hasten where
The old yule-log is burning.
And where at night the ruddy light
Of that old log is flinging

A genial joy o'er girl and boy,
There I resume my singing.

And, when they hear my chirrup clear,
The children stop their playing—
With eager feet they haste to greet
My welcome music, saying:
"The little thing has come to sing
Of woodland, hedge, and thicket—
Of summer day and lambs at play—
Oh, how we love the cricket!"

"This merry little song always seemed to please everybody except the gnat. The fairies appeared to regard the gnat as a pestiferous insect, but a contemptuous pity led them to call upon him for a recitation, which invariably was in the following strain:

THE FATE OF THE FLIMFLAM

A flimflam flopped from a fillamaloo,
Where the pollywog pinkled so pale,
And the pipkin piped a petulant "pooh"
 To the garrulous gawp of the gale.
"Oh, woe to the swap of the sweeping swipe
That booms on the hobbling bay!"
Snickered the snark to the snoozing snipe
That lurked where the lamprey lay.

The gluglug glinked in the glimmering gloam,
Where the buzbuz bumbled his bee—
When the flimflam flitted, all flecked with foam,
From the sozzling and succulent sea.
 "Oh, swither the swipe, with its sweltering sweep!"
She swore as she swayed in a swoon,
And a doleful dank dumped over the deep,
To the lay of the limpid loon!

 "This was simply horrid, as you all will allow. The queen and her fairy followers were much relieved when the honest katydid narrated a pleasant moral in the form of a ballad to this effect:

CONTENTMENT

Once on a time an old red hen
Went strutting 'round with pompous clucks,
For she had little babies ten,
A part of which were tiny ducks.
"'T is very rare that hens," said she,
"Have baby ducks as well as chicks—
But I possess, as you can see,
Of chickens four and ducklings six!"

A season later, this old hen

Appeared, still cackling of her luck,
For, though she boasted babies ten,
Not one among them was a duck!
"T is well," she murmured, brooding o'er
The little chicks of fleecy down—
"My babies now will stay ashore,
And, consequently, cannot drown!"

The following spring the old red hen
Clucked just as proudly as of yore—
But lo! her babes were ducklings ten,
Instead of chickens, as before!
"T is better," said the old red hen,
As she surveyed her waddling brood;
"A little water now and then
Will surely do my darlings good!"

But oh! alas, how very sad!
When gentle spring rolled round again
The eggs eventuated bad,
And childless was the old red hen!
Yet patiently she bore her woe,
And still she wore a cheerful air,
And said: "'T is best these things are so,
For babies are a dreadful care!"

I half suspect that many men,
And many, many women, too,
Could learn a lesson from the hen
With foliage of vermilion hue;
She ne'er presumed to take offence
At any fate that might befall,
But meekly bowed to Providence—
She was contented—that was all!

"Then the fairies would resume their dancing. Each little gentleman fairy would bow to his lady fairy and sing in the most musical of voices:

Sweet little fairy,
Tender and airy,
Come, let us dance on the good baby-eyes;
Merrily skipping,
Cheerily tripping,
Murmur we ever our soft lullabies.

"And then, as the rest danced, the fairy queen sang the following slumber-song, accompanied by the orchestra:

A FAIRY LULLABY

There are two stars in yonder steeps

That watch the baby while he sleeps.
But while the baby is awake
And singing gayly all day long,
The little stars their slumbers take
Lulled by the music of his song.
So sleep, dear tired baby, sleep
While little stars their vigils keep.

Beside his loving mother-sheep
A little lambkin is asleep;
What does he know of midnight gloom—
He sleeps, and in his quiet dreams
He thinks he plucks the clover bloom
And drinks at cooling, purling streams.
And those same stars the baby knows
Sing softly to the lamb's repose.

Sleep, little lamb; sleep, little child—
The stars are dim—the night is wild;
But o'er the cot and o'er the lea
A sleepless eye forever beams—
A shepherd watches over thee
In all thy little baby dreams;
The shepherd loves his tiny sheep—
Sleep, precious little lambkin, sleep!

"That is very pretty, indeed!" exclaimed the brass candlestick.

"So it is," replied the little shoe, "but you should hear it sung by the fairy queen!"

"Did the operetta end with that lullaby?" inquired the cigar-case.

"Oh, no," said the little shoe. "No sooner had the queen finished her lullaby than an old gran'ma fairy, wearing a quaint mob-cap and large spectacles, limped forward with her crutch and droned out a curious ballad, which seemed to be for the special benefit of the boy and girl fairies, very many of whom were of the company. This ballad was as follows:

BALLAD OF THE JELLY-CAKE

A little boy whose name was Tim
Once ate some jelly-cake for tea—
Which cake did not agree with him,
As by the sequel you shall see.
"My darling child," his mother said,
"Pray do not eat that jelly-cake,
For, after you have gone to bed,
I fear 't will make your stomach ache!"
But foolish little Tim demurred
Unto his mother's warning word.

That night, while all the household slept,

Tim felt an awful pain, and then
From out the dark a nightmare leapt
And stood upon his abdomen!
"I cannot breathe!" the infant cried—
"Oh, Mrs. Nightmare, pity take!"
"There is no mercy," she replied,
"For boys who feast on jelly-cake!"
And so, despite the moans of Tim,
The cruel nightmare went for him.

At first, she 'd tickle Timmy's toes
Or roughly smite his baby cheek—
And now she 'd rudely tweak his nose
And other petty vengeance wreak;
And then, with hobnails in her shoes
And her two horrid eyes aflame,
The mare proceeded to amuse
Herself by prancing o'er his frame—-
First to his throbbing brow, and then
Back to his little feet again.

At last, fantastic, wild, and weird,
And clad in garments ghastly grim,
A scowling hoodoo band appeared
And joined in worrying little Tim.
Each member of this hoodoo horde
Surrounded Tim with fierce ado
And with long, cruel gimlets bored
His aching system through and through,
And while they labored all night long
The nightmare neighed a dismal song.

Next morning, looking pale and wild,
Poor little Tim emerged from bed—
"Good gracious! what can ail the child!"
His agitated mother said.
"We live to learn," responded he,
"And I have lived to learn to take
Plain bread and butter for my tea,
And never, never, jelly-cake!
For when my hulk with pastry teems,
I must expect unpleasant dreams!"

"Now you can imagine this ballad impressed the child fairies very deeply," continued the little shoe. "Whenever the gran'ma fairy sang it, the little fairies expressed great surprise that boys and girls ever should think of eating things which occasioned so much trouble. So the night was spent in singing and dancing, and our master would sleep as sweetly as you please. At last the lark—what a beautiful bird she is—would flutter against the window panes, and give the fairies warning in these words:

MORNING SONG

The eastern sky is streaked with red,
The weary night is done,
And from his distant ocean bed
Rolls up the morning sun.
The dew, like tiny silver beads
Bespread o'er velvet green,
Is scattered on the wakeful meads
By angel hands unseen.
"Good-morrow, robin in the trees!"
The star-eyed daisy cries;
"Good-morrow," sings the morning breeze
Unto the ruddy skies;
"Good-morrow, every living thing!"
Kind Nature seems to say,
And all her works devoutly sing
A hymn to birth of day,
So, haste, without delay,
Haste, fairy friends, on silver wing,
And to your homes away!

"But the fairies could never leave little master so unceremoniously. Before betaking themselves to their pretty homes under the rocks near the brook, they would address a parting song to his eyes, and this song they called a matin invocation:

TO A SLEEPING BABY'S EYES

And thou, twin orbs of love and joy!
Unveil thy glories with the morn—
Dear eyes, another day is born—
Awake, O little sleeping boy!
Bright are the summer morning skies,
But in this quiet little room
There broods a chill, oppressive gloom—
All for the brightness of thine eyes.
Without those radiant orbs of thine
How dark this little world would be—
This sweet home-world that worships thee—
So let their wondrous glories shine
On those who love their warmth and joy—
Awake, O sleeping little boy.

"So that ended the fairy operetta, did it?" inquired the match-box.

"Yes," said the little shoe, with a sigh of regret. "The fairies were such bewitching creatures, and they sang so sweetly, I could have wished they would never stop their antics and singing. But, alas! I fear I shall never see them again."

"What makes you think so?" asked the brass candlestick.

"I 'm sure I can't tell," replied the little shoe; "only everything is so strange-like and so changed from what it used to be that I hardly know whether indeed I am still the same little shoe I used to be."

"Why, what can you mean?" queried the old clock, with a puzzled look on her face.

"I will try to tell you," said the little shoe. "You see, my mate and our master and I were great friends; as I have said, we roamed and frolicked around together all day, and at night my little mate and I watched at master's bedside while he slept. One day we three took a long ramble, away up the street and beyond where the houses were built, until we came into a beautiful green field, where the grass was very tall and green, and where there were pretty flowers of every kind. Our little master talked to the flowers and they answered him, and we all had a merry time in the meadow that afternoon, I can tell you. 'Don't go away, little child,' cried the daisies, 'but stay and be our playfellow always.' A butterfly came and perched on our master's hand, and looked up and smiled, and said: 'I 'm not afraid of you; you would n't hurt me, would you?' A little mouse told us there was a thrush's nest in the bush yonder, and we hurried to see it. The lady thrush was singing her four babies to sleep. They were strange-looking babies, with their gaping mouths, bulbing eyes, and scant feathers! 'Do not wake them up,' protested the lady thrush. 'Go a little further on and you will come to the brook. I will join you presently.' So we went to the brook."

"Oh, but I would have been afraid," suggested the pen-wiper.

"Afraid of the brook!" cried the little shoe. "Oh, no; what could be prettier than the brook! We heard it singing in the distance. We called to it and it bade us welcome. How it smiled in the sunshine! How restless and furtive and nimble it was, yet full of merry prattling and noisy song. Our master was overjoyed. He had never seen the brook before; nor had we, for that matter. 'Let me cool your little feet,' said the brook, and, without replying, our master waded knee-deep into the brook. In an instant we were wet through—my mate and I; but how deliciously cool it was here in the brook, and how smooth and bright the pebbles were! One of the pebbles told me it had come many, many miles that day from its home in the hills where the brook was born."

"Pooh, I don't believe it," sneered the vase.

"Presently our master toddled back from out the brook," continued the little shoe, heedless of the vase's interruption, "and sat among the cowslips and buttercups on the bank. The brook sang on as merrily as before. 'Would you like to go sailing?' asked our master of my mate. 'Indeed I would,' replied my mate, and so our master pulled my mate from his little foot and set it afloat upon the dancing waves of the brook. My mate was not the least alarmed. It spun around gayly several times at first and then glided rapidly away. The butterfly hastened and alighted upon the merry little craft. 'Where are you going?' I cried. 'I am going down to the sea,' replied my little mate, with laughter. 'And I am going to marry the rose in the far-away south,' cried the butterfly. 'But will you not come back?' I cried. They answered me, but they were so far away I could not hear them. It was very distressing, and I grieved exceedingly. Then, all at once, I discovered my little master was asleep, fast asleep among the cowslips and buttercups. I did not try to wake him—only I felt very miserable, for I was so cold and wet. Presently the lady thrush came, as she had said she would. The child is asleep— he will be ill—I must hasten to tell his mother,' she cried, and away she flew."

"And was he sick?" asked the vase.

"I do not know," said the little shoe. "I can remember it was late that evening when the sweet lady and others came and took us up and carried us back home, to this very room. Then I was pulled off very unceremoniously and thrown under my little master's bed, and I never saw my little master after that.

"How very strange!" exclaimed the match-safe.

"Very, very strange," repeated the shoe. "For many days and nights I lay under the crib all alone. I could hear my little master sighing and talking as if in a dream. Sometimes he spoke of me, and of the brook, and of my little mate dancing to the sea, and one night he breathed very loud and quick and he cried out and seemed to struggle, and then, all at once, he stopped, and I could hear the sweet lady weeping. But I remember all this very faintly. I was hoping the fairies would come back, but they never came.

"I remember," resumed the little shoe, after a solemn pause, "I remember how, after a long, long time, the sweet lady came and drew me from under the crib and held me in her lap and kissed me and wept over me. Then she put me in a dark, lonesome drawer, where there were dresses and stockings and the little hat my master used to wear. There I lived, oh! such a weary time, and we talked—the dresses, the stockings, the hat, and I did—about our little master, and we wondered that he never came. And every little while the sweet lady would take us from the drawer and caress us, and we saw that she was pale and that her eyes were red with weeping."

"But has your little master never come back!" asked the old clock.

"Not yet," said the little shoe, "and that is why I am so very lonesome. Sometimes I think he has gone down to the sea in search of my little mate and that the two will come back together. But I do not understand it. The sweet lady took me from the drawer to-day and kissed me and set me here on the mantelpiece."

"You don't mean to say she kissed you?" cried the haughty vase, "you horrid little stumped-out shoe!"

"Indeed she did," insisted the lonesome little shoe, "and I know she loves me. But why she loves me and kisses me and weeps over me I do not know. It is all very strange. I do not understand it at all."

Eugene Field – A Short Biography

Eugene Field was born on 2nd September, 1850 in St. Louis, Missouri at 634 S. Broadway to parents Roswell Martin and Frances Reed Field, both of New England stock. Tragically Field lost his mother at age 6 and was thereafter brought up by a cousin, Mary Field French, in Amherst, Massachusetts.

Field attended Williams College in Williamstown, Massachusetts.

When he was 19 his father died, and Field dropped out of Williams. Field's father, Roswell Martin Field, was the lawyer for Dred Scott, the slave who famously sued for his freedom. The complaint was sometimes referred to as 'The lawsuit that started the Civil War'.

Field then went to Knox College in Galesburg, Illinois, but again dropped out. This time after a year. However he did then summon himself to attend the University of Missouri in Columbia, Missouri, where his brother Roswell was studying. As can be gathered from his efforts to date Field was not the most serious of students but was gaining the reputation of being a prankster. Among his more outlandish attempts were a raid on the president's wine cellar, painting the president's house in school colors, and firing the school's landmark cannons at midnight.

Field tried acting but found it not to his liking, studied law but with little success, but did have an interest in writing for the student newspaper.

When his studies finished in 1871, although he never graduated, he collected his share of his inheritance from his father's estate, and set off for a trip to explore Europe. After six months, with funds from the inheritance exhausted, he returned to the United States.

Field then set to work as a journalist for the St. Joseph Gazette in Saint Joseph, Missouri, in 1875.

That same year he married the sixteen-year-old Julia Sutherland Comstock of St Joseph, Missouri. They would eventually have eight children during their twenty-two years of marriage, of whom only five would reach adulthood. Field, knowing that his understanding of finances was somewhat poor, arranged for all the money he earned to be sent to his wife for her to administer on behalf of the family.

In his career as a journalist he soon found a niche that suited him. His articles were light, humorous and written in a personal and gossipy style that endeared him to his readership. Some were soon being syndicated to other newspapers around the States. Field rose to be the city editor of the Gazette.

From 1876 through 1880, the Family lived in St. Louis. Field worked initially as an editorial writer for the Morning Journal and then for the Times-Journal. From there he worked for a short time as the managing editor of the Kansas City Times before settling, for two years, as the editor of the Denver Tribune. He also wrote a column for the paper, 'Odds and Ends,' poking fun at the climate, the muddy roads, the frontier language, and other aspects of Denver life. However his readership was large and growing. Further opportunities would come.

In 1883 the Field moved the family to Chicago lured by a salary of $50 a week. Field now began work for the Chicago Daily News. Here he wrote his humorous newspaper column called Sharps and Flats. He quickly found out that $50 dollars in Denver didn't stretch that far in bustling Chicago.

His column ran in the newspaper's morning edition. In it Field made quips about issues and personalities of the day, especially regarding the arts and literature. His pet subject was the intellectual superiority of Chicago, especially when he compared it to Boston, which he often did. In April 1887, he wrote, "While Chicago is humping herself in the interests of literature, art and the sciences, vain old Boston is frivoling away her precious time in an attempted renaissance of the cod fisheries."

In another article that year after Chicago's National League baseball club sold future baseball Hall of Famer Mike "King" Kelly to Boston which overlapped with a speaking tour visit from the famous Boston poet and diplomat James Russell Lowell he wrote: "Chicago feels a special interest in Mr. Lowell at this particular time because he is perhaps the foremost representative of the enterprising and opulent community which within the last week has secured the services of one of Chicago's honored sons for the base-ball season of 1887. The fact that Boston has come to Chicago for the captain of her baseball nine has reinvigorated the bonds of affection between the metropolis of the Bay state and the metropolis of the mighty west; the truth of this will appear in the mighty welcome which our public will give Mr. Lowell next Tuesday."

It was in 1888 that his poem 'Little Boy Blue' was printed in America, a weekly journal. It achieved for Field instant and lasting fame. Coincidentally the same issue carried a poem by James Russell Lowell. Field was immensely pleased that his own poem was regarded with considerably more weight and acclaim.

Field had first published poetry in 1879, when his poem 'Christmas Treasures' was published. It later appeared in 'A Little Book of Western Verse' (1889). This was the beginning that would eventually number over a dozen volumes. He developed a style of light-hearted poems for children. Among the perennial favorites are 'Wynken, Blynken, and Nod' and 'The Duel' (but better known as 'The Gingham Dog and the Calico Cat') and 'Little Boy Blue' about the death of a child. As well as verse Field published an extensive range of short stories including 'The Holy Cross' and 'Daniel and the Devil.'

Field treasured rare, unusual and beautiful books and his personal library had scores of them. He also enjoyed making them too and frequently worked long hours with great care and various colored inks decorating the first letter of his poems.

In 1889 whilst the family were in London and Field himself was recovering from a bout of ill health he wrote his most famous poem; 'Lovers Lane'. It is often thought to have been written whilst the couple were courting but recent research settles it authorship to this later date. The poem was written as a reminder of better days when the couple courted in her father's buggy on 'Lover's Lane, St Jo'.

Field was ever curious and keen to push his boundaries. In 1891 with his brother Roswell they wrote and published 'Echoes from the Sabine Farm' a loosely translated version of Horace.

On 4th November 1895 Eugene Field Sr died in Chicago of a heart attack at the age of 45. He is buried at the Church of the Holy Comforter in Kenilworth, Illinois.

The New York Times described his death: CHICAGO, Nov. 4. — Eugene Field, the poet and humorist, died at 5 o'clock this morning of heart disease at his residence in Buena Park. Although Mr. Field had been ill for the past three days, his sudden death was totally unexpected.

Field was originally interred at Graceland Cemetery in Chicago, but his son-in-law, Senior Warden of the Church of the Holy Comforter, had him reinterred on 7th March, 1926.

Several of his poems were set to music with commercial success. Many of his works were accompanied by paintings from the exceptional talents of Maxfield Parrish.

During his lifetime he was often referred to as the 'poet of childhood'. This may account for his anonymous publication of 'Only a Boy'. In our own times the work would probably be frowned upon. It concerns a 12-year-old boy being seduced by a woman in her 30s. The 1920's drama critic/magazine editor George Jean Nathan claimed it was a popular but forbidden work among those coming of age in the early 1900's.

Much of what Field wrote was light, humourous and of its time. And that is perhaps why it has endured. Its writes of a time that, in his words, suspends itself from the harsh reality of real life to a gentler and more touching time that exists in the imagination.

The Tribune Primer (1882)
Culture's Garland (1887)
A Little Book of Profitable Tales (1889)
A Little Book of Western Verse (1889)
With Trumpet and Drum (1892)
Echoes from the Sabine Farm (1893)
The Holy Cross and Other Tales (1893)
Second Book of Verse (1893)
Love Songs of Childhood (1894)
Love Affairs of a Bibliomaniac (1895)
Little Willie (1895)
Songs and Other Verse (1896)
Second Book of Tales (1896)
The House; An Episode in the Lives of Reuben Baker, Astronomer and His Wife Alice (1896)
Field Flowers (1896)
Florence Bardsley's Story (1897)
Lullaby Songs of Childhood (1897)
Lullaby Land (1898)
Sharps and Flats (1900)
The Stars (1901)
Nonsense for Old and Young (1901)
A Little Book of Nonsense (1901)
A Little Book of Tribune Verse (1901)
The Sabine Farm (1903)
John Smith USA (1905)
The Clink of Ice (1905)
Hoosier Lyrics (1905)
Cradle Lullabies (1909)
The Poems of Eugene Field (1910)
Christmas Tales and Christmas Verse (1912)
Penn-Yan Bill's Wooing (1914)
The Yankee Abroad (1917)
The Mouse and the Moonbeam (1919)
Poems of Childhood (1920)
The Gingham Dog and the Calico Cat (1926)
Child Verses (1927)
The Sugar Plum Tree (1929)
In Wink-a-way Land (1930)